SURGE

surge; *noun*

a sudden powerful forward or upward movement, especially by a
crowd or by a natural force such as the tide.
'flooding caused by tidal surges'

SURGE

INTRODUCTION
BY FRANK
McGUINNESS

NEW WRITING
FROM
IRELAND

BRANDON
AN IMPRINT OF O'BRIEN

First published 2014 by Brandon,
an imprint of The O'Brien Press Ltd,
12 Terenure Road East, Rathgar,
Dublin 6, Ireland.
Tel: +353 1 4923333; Fax: +353 1 4922777
Email: books@obrien.ie
Website: www.obrien.ie

ISBN: 978-1-84717-693-6

1 3 5 7 8 6 4 2
14 16 18 19 17 15

Printed and bound by CPI Group (UK) Ltd, Croydon, CR0 4YY.
The paper in this book is produced using pulp from managed forests.

The O'Brien Press receives
financial assistance from

LOTTERY FUNDED

CONTENTS

INTRODUCTION

SURGE

NOTES ON CONTRIBUTORS

INDEX OF AUTHORS BY UNIVERSITY

WHY SURGE?

MICHAEL O'BRIEN

My father, who founded The O'Brien Press with me forty years ago, also helped to found the New Theatre Group, in 1937. A radical theatre, it played in Dublin's Peacock and other small theatres. The NTG's magazine was *Surge*, and it published new fiction, poems, novel extracts, short stories and political and dramatic commentary and review.

In March 1943, my father wrote in *Surge* about the ideals of the NTG's founders and its future: 'There was an extraordinary spirit, a creative will-to-do … Its purpose was to give to its socialist progressive audience plays that no other Irish theatre dared produce … to play a serious role in the dramatic role of the nation.' He continued: 'It must find its own national playwrights and it must produce their plays in a theatre which is capable of paying royalties and wages.' A similar spirit has surrounded The O'Brien Press since it published its first books in November 1974.

The idea of a short story collection showcasing the best emerging Irish talent was first raised at a board meeting of the Dublin Book Festival. Ireland has a great tradition for the short story, which flourished in the 1940s and 50s when *The Bell* magazine, edited by Sean O'Faoláin, Peadar O'Donnell and Anthony Cronin, discovered and published the creative talent of the era. As part of our Brandon Fiction programme, O'Brien Press wished to bring together new talent from all parts of modern Ireland, and found inspiration in the current work of the creative writing schools in the four green fields of our major universities. For the collection, we decided not to separate the authors into their individual colleges, nor to arrange them by alphabetical order of surname. By what logic or theme are the stories arranged? That is for the reader to work out.

It's a joy to work with so many creative and inspiring people in the five universities: National University of Ireland, Galway (Adrian Frazier, John Kenny, Mike McCormack, Lionel Pilkington, Julia Kilroy); Queen's University Belfast (Glenn Patterson, Darran McCann, Garrett Carr, Ciaran Carson); Trinity College Dublin (Gerald Dawe, Deirdre Madden, Gina Moxley); University College Cork (Mary Morrissy, Claire Connolly, Eibhear Walshe); and University College Dublin (Frank McGuinness, Éilís Ní Dhuibhne, James Ryan). There is a real feeling of partnership in the writing, making and promoting of *Surge*. So thank you, writers, students, leaders and teachers, with a special thanks to Frank McGuinness for his fine introduction and for inspiring support for *Surge*, Brandon and The O'Brien Press - a true friend.

Thanks also to our wonderful staff, authors, artists, industry colleagues, the Arts Council and Northern Ireland Arts Council, Dublin Book Festival, Patrick Sutton and Smock Alley Theatre, media, readers and all who helped with this unique project.

Launching *Surge* in November 2014 at Dublin Book Festival in Smock Alley Theatre marks forty years of O'Brien and the 100th anniversary of my father, Tom O'Brien's, birth. I'm proud to hand on the *Surge* title to a new generation of creative writers, and I hope it truly carries forward the best of what we have achieved over forty years.

BRICK

FRANK McGuinness

I know a woman who flung a brick through her partner's window. When confronted why, she explained she wanted to make sure they would answer the door – there were times you had to do more than knock. I find that incident an inspiration. While the most adroit of writers in this genre can achieve effects of breathtaking subtlety, I'd still maintain in every successful short story you can find, among delicate shards of glass, that solid brick, threatening, wonderful, ready to propel itself, if necessary, into one's imagination, doing damage, external and internal, and, unlike most novels, not remotely bothered to care what consequent healing may be necessary. There is then a ruthlessness about the form, and its style is a matter of how that ruthlessness disguises itself.

The stories in this collection come from students in creative-writing courses at master's level in Queen's University Belfast; Trinity College, Dublin; University College Cork; National

University of Ireland, Galway; and University College Dublin. Two students from each institution have submitted work, as has a mentor of their writing. I am not going to spoil any shocks or spike any guns loaded within by detailing plots or revealing characters that populate these pages, but I will say if this assembly proves anything, it is that, even on the most cursory of readings, there is evidence of a remarkable complexity and sophistication of voices and visions emerging out of our colleges. Each story surprises by reason of its difference from what proceeds and precedes it in the order of the book. Taken together, these fictions entertain like the best of conversations, each woman and man holding their own corner, saying what it is they have to say, and not one outstaying their welcome. They know by instinct how to keep their counsel, most tantalisingly and most beguilingly when they really should not do so, leaving the reader's tongue hanging out for more, and, with genuinely Irish hospitality, not obliging.

There is nothing worse than a story overstuffing itself. No fear of that here. This is writing that marks austere times by its economy, and so it proves itself to be all the more genuinely sympathetic to those afflicted by the history, past, present and to come, of that financial deluge. Every single piece of fiction here in its diverse way stands as a metaphor of the profound change, the seismic change, our culture has undergone these past years. Wounds, visible and invisible, are detected; their trauma is the touch from which there is no recovery. In the best possible sense, this is art of its time.

And the old school out there will surely be delighted that these folk provide sound moral guidance to all aspiring writers. What is this moral? Find your brick, smash a window, leg it. The window should, of course, be your own, so return to collect and do what you must with its pieces.

BIRTHDAY BOYS

FERGUS CRONIN

The two dogs stop their yapping and look over at me from the shed across the yard. Baleful. They won't come across in this rain. Are they wondering how I'll open this door? No latch, just a bit of rope. Typical. Hit it with the shoulder anyway. Gust blows me in. Feckin rain follows me in too. Shut it out with a slam of the arse. Throw on a light. No sign of the quare lad, or that other hobo. Table in disarray, embers smouldering, kettle as black as Nigeria. Sootwebs for decoration on the mantel. Two black cats on a dirty old mat … only see their yellow eyes. The old farmhouse has three rooms. This middle room is where everything happens. Has done for one, two hundred years. See the crib is in place, on top of the old food safe. Normal so.

Shake out the hair.

'I'd say you didn't trim it since.'

'You fecker … I didn't see you.'

'Happy Christmas so, little brother.'

'Ah yeh, the same to yourself. Jeez, Nog, what's that you have?'

I've called him Nog since I was a child and couldn't get my tongue around his full Christian. Saved him from an eternal Nollaig. He has come from the dark cave that is his bedroom, holding some class of a coloured paper decoration which he goes to pin up over the hearth.

'Ah for feck's sake look at your own. Is it dreads you have it in or is it just more soot?'

A white gap opens in his gaunt bristly face and he makes the silent laugh with his great bulgy eyes. His long dreadlocks are gathered in at the neck and slung inside a grimy collar.

'My sootlocks. Hah. Did you throw your head into Little Andy's? Any sign of the other honch? On the road?'

'Nah, I walked straight up from the bus. Terrible crossing earlier. Set off the alarm at security. Is he about?'

'I haven't seen him, but I hear he's around okay. Stoppin over at Delia's, I'm told. Last couple of nights.'

Typical JJ. He's the middle brother. Have to smile.

'He'll have had the Beatle boots off so. And polished?'

'Did you notice a black one out on the acre? I can't see her in the back field and I was waiting for it to stop peltin. She'd be heavy.'

'Can't say I did.'

'It's comin in hard all right. You came up with it against you.

She'd be stupid enough to turn into it too. Go on up, into it.'

'I can't say I'd any choice in the matter and there isn't a leaf on a tree.'

'Don't be touchy. I was sayin that she's stupid. I'll get her when it stops.'

'I'd say it's down for the evening. You still keeping them on so?'

'Ah, a couple, for the, you know, grant or whatever. The payment yoke from Europe. Know the feck. Reps. Europe be the feck.'

Nog had got the bit of land after the father had shagged off. Then he had stayed on with Mama, until she went. We brought her ashes home ten years ago tomorrow, on Christmas Day.

My oldest brother is a peculiar man; like the rest of us I suppose. He spends half his time gadding about the country – after theatre and art, the heck. The rest he stays here, and I suppose keeps it up. The other lad wanders about in some other direction picking up a gig here and there. JJ was in bands – showbands, rock bands – so he has his circuit. Me? In a peculiar way, I'm probably the most settled. I've lived in London for, oh, over forty years now. Started life as a class of a hippy, then tried the political stuff: you know, the revolution – where did that feck off to? Sure I got pissed off with it anyway, with Thatcher you know, so I became a punk. Feck me. Then I retired and got a job in the Council and settled down to a sweet life of work, blues, ganja and healthy food, all by my lonesome. Oh, and grew the hair again. We all do now. It's something for Mama. Swore one Christmas we'd never cut it again, none of us. Mama loved that. Her three hairy crows. Feck the rest of them.

Growing up in our house we all read our share. Mama's people were townies, teachers and the like, so she came stocked. The father read his own stuff: the *Irish Press*, *Reader's Digest*. Mama swore that she got him to read Turgenev. Maybe that's why he fecked off. Nog can't remember that, but then there is a lot to forget too. Every year I bring them a book each – slim, so as not to burden them in their travels. Poetry is ideal. In fairness, you would hardly think of either of them that way – if you didn't know them that is. They are both big, strong, wild-looking men. Yeh, but how shall I put it … they have their sensitive side. JJ might draw a clout now and again – well able to – but we are all of us passive men beneath. Myself, I am of a weaker construction, being short and slight, but I have been described as wiry, and that gets me by.

'You'll like that, I think. She's the Poet Laureate now. It's a good one to carry around.'

'Thanks, brother. That's brillant. Here, did I tell you about that feckin Beckett play I saw up in Dublin?'

The table is cleared back a little and tea and a couple of egg sandwiches are set up. Nog is splayed on the chair with no back, having left the one with the back to me, his gesture to my weaker frame. When JJ joins us he can use the crate.

'It was that one with the pair in the dustbins. *The Endgame*. What? Jaze, I'll tell you, it was brillant! Brillant altogether. And a laugh. Oh, a feckin great laugh. Did you ever come over it? You should. I was up for a week in the hostel, there in Amiens Street. A great breakfast. I went across to that art gallery. Saw that painter buck O'Donoghue's pictures on the Way of the Cross. Brillant.'

'I see you have the crib up.'

'I do. Tradition. Hah?'

'Tradition. Yeh, I suppose. We'll all go up to the graveyard tomorrow as per usual? Are you ready this year? Any news on a headstone?'

'Nah. Didn't get back to your man. Still, he has the piece of marble got. From feckin China no less. What the feck. Hey.'

'Hey, what?'

'Hey, look what the wind blew in now. Howya buck? I was just sayin to me other buck here that the feckin marble comes in from China now.'

'What feckin marble?'

'For the grave above.'

'Sure there's no one up there.'

JJ's giving it the usual rattle. He is looking good. Great man for the suit. This time a pinstripe no less. No way am I sure about the plum shirt though. Looks like something from one of his showbands. Sure, probably is. His hair down over his shoulders in a soaked black sheen. How does he keep the colour I wonder? Although, in fairness now, he could be a man for the dye. And sure Nog the same, but he's definitely not a man for the dye. Mine all gone grey and these two bucks, ten, and what, twelve years older, and all black. I look at the kettle. Yeh, it must be from me living in the city. JJ throws down an old saxophone case and goes over to the fireplace where Nog has got a blaze lit.

'Good to see the old crib out. Tradition.'

'Yeh, me and Nog were just saying about going up to the grave tomorrow.'

'Like I was saying: there's no one up there.'

In fairness he was right. Mama's ashes haven't been taken up yet. Her own folk didn't want her back, so where else is there to put her? Sure what the feck else would we be talking about doing on Christmas Day anyway. I look to see what Nog will say. He's holding back, looking at his poetry book, shaping to ignore the trend that is coming about. JJ is looking into the fireplace and saying it – the thing he always brings out.

'So I'll say it again. Isn't it way past time we brought up them ol' ashes and buried, or scattered, or whatever you're supposed to do with 'em? Nog? We say this every year, and there's always some ol' reason. Didn't you say last year that you'd be ready? That you'd have the headstone and some ol' prayer or a poem or something sorted for this year?'

I have to agree with JJ. He's turned now from the fire, and I can see into his big smoky eyes and the look is determined.

There'll be no dodging this bullet, I'm thinking. No, not this year. The both of us are now looking over at Nog, who looks up, after a steady little wait. There we are: the three shaggy heads all looking at each other. Three shaggy feckers under a tin lid that keeps us dry. Then Nog looks over at the crib.

'All right. We'll do it so.'

Christmas morning, and the yard is flooded, but the rain has stopped and the day is cold and bright. The watery light in the room is coming in over the books that are packed in the deep sill of the back window. Nog comes in, all business, in his wellingtons, with the tops rolled down. Funny I think; he's like Noah, with his pairs of dogs, cows, cats … and brothers. He is in and out doing fiddly bits and pieces all morning, and we chat away between mouthfuls of breakfast.

A half dozen fried eggs have been polished off, and a whiff of burning turf and grease hangs in the air by the time JJ surfaces after twelve. His suit is all crumpled. There isn't a whole lot of talk out of him. He goes straight over to the crib and looks in at it for a while. It's a simple affair, made up of a cardboard box on its side and covered in a kind of black crinkly paper. The opening like the mouth of hell itself with a fairy light giving off a red glow from inside. I expect to hear water dripping. Well, there was always a drip from somewhere. 'Hey, did you fix all them leaks or what?'

The crib has never changed, not since I can remember. Like the house – other than the thatch is off now. The tin up and the new toilet tacked on to the back wall. I look into the maw of the crib. There's the baby, a baby king with his crown and his other king things; the world and the wand yoke held splayed out, his little legs crossed. A snatch of straw, kept from the old roof, makes up the little manger for the baby to lie in.

That Christmas we brought the ashes home, we divided them up in three. We'd each of us had the fill of one of Nog's Old Holborn tins. The idea, I suppose, was that we'd each of us have our own, well, piece of Mama, to keep in comfort … our own way. Whatever about anyone else's, it was always understood that the home ashes, Nog's, would be properly buried or whatever, in case anyone was ever coming back – say after we'd all be gone – you know, to pray or whatever. Visit. The other two-thirds of Mama could wander around with JJ and myself, as I said, for comfort. Nog kept dragging his heels on it, but sure something would have to give; we needed to put some of Mama to rest. Anyway, that was the sum of it.

My own tin was always sitting there, on a table or a shelf, wherever I fetched up. Well, actually, I had moved them for a while to a wooden box that Sha, fuck, had given me. It came from India I think. I used to keep my dope in it … then my mama. For a while I had a little, like, holy cloth over it and would often uncover it and light a candle and a few joss sticks and play

'My Sweet Lord', that George Harrison song. A little ceremony. Out of it. Oh yeh, tears. Back safe in the tin now though.

Don't know what's the story with JJ's. Things have a habit of detaching themselves from that man. Like he leaves things in places. Doesn't really lose stuff, just moves on without it. And then, usually, the stuff catches up, somehow. Used to keep the tin in that old sax case. That's always somewhere he can get at it, has to be if he gets a gig. Has it with him now. Wonder if the tin's still in it? Of course he might have tried to shove them up his nose too. He'll play something if we ever get graveside. Remember him blowing that thing when he was a kid. Fourteen, fifteen, whatever. I must have been five or six. Loved the sound. Blues. Mama got him those American records in Cork. The father used to say he'd be better off with the cattle in the house. Maybe that's what drove the old man away. Left when I was ten. One day he was just … not there. I can only remember Mama hugging me and she not crying at all. No tears, just a surge of energy in the house. Nog was around but seemed to be out always, away in a far field. He never spoke about it then, or now. JJ was already gone with the bands.

It's getting late in the day, and we are waiting for Nog to come out of the toilet so's we can get the show on the road. JJ and myself have found old wellies, and now we're like navvies waiting for a pick, the tops of our boots turned down, like Nog. JJ, in his suit, looks like a construction boss and is getting on to Nog again. He shouts in at him. 'Well, for feck's sake. How much can a man piss?'

'Will you hould your donkey out there. I was out of paper.'

'And what did you use. Ya dirty—'

'I've a stack of old Musical Expressos that I'm workin through …'

'Ya feck, they're mine.'

Nog is out now, beaming.

'Will ya feck off. I've other bog rolls, just couldn't put my hands on em, and, when I did … let's say they were damp. But I didn't use your feckin old *NME*s, haven't a notion where they are.'

'And you used damp bog roll?'

'Yeh?'

'You're a feckin animal. What are yeh?'

Nog is giddy now, laughing, and he grabs JJ into a headlock. JJ is scuffling about, banging Nog's legs with a fist, laughing even louder. They bang on into the food safe, and the crib starts to rock. I grab at it and stop it falling. A shepherd tumbles out onto the stone floor and loses its head. The tiny sound of plaster snapping stills the commotion.

'Ah, for feck's sake, men.'

Nog lets JJ out, and then his big black head pushes past me. He is looking into the crib, all concerned. His massive hands reach in, gently lifting the baby and taking an Old Holborn tin from under the straw. He leaves the baby back down and carries the tin, cupped in his hands, slowly to the table. His eyes, all soft, are on the tin, as he brings it into the last of the sunbeams from the back window. Rust marks streak the orange and white cover and the brassy box of the tin. He sets it down gently. It looks at home there on the faded pattern of the creamy oilcloth, among the egg stains and breadcrumbs. JJ has straightened himself and come around to look. We all lean in over the little tin. Nothing needs to be said. We've each of us perfected our silent prayer over the long years.

Outside, the ground is saturated, but the air is crisp and the blue of the sky is paling; shortly, it will deepen into sunset. We leave the yard and fall into single file for the march up the hill to the graveyard. Nog leads, JJ in the middle with his sax case and me bringing up the rear. There are only a few houses on either side in the half mile up. It being Christmas Day, each is its own oasis of warmth and peace. This is the day when everyone is in. Even from the road you can feel the ease that has entered these simple cottages. Coloured lights sparkle: inside on trees and outside on eaves and walls and trees again. There is a glow from the TVs.

There was never a television brought into our house, but we always had the best of fare at Christmas. Mama saw to that: good food, drink, when we were old enough, and reading and talk. Debate was what she lived for. Rights and wrongs. Ins and outs. So, no matter that our schooling ended early (only I finished secondary), we all three had gone into the world wisened up because of Mama. No doubt that each of us is thinking something like that as we go on up.

'They'll all be lookin at the three of us now. Pass no heed.'

Nog is not meaning to be unfriendly; he is just minding our attempt at being, well, solemn. Yeh. I imagine there are signals of goodwill towards us from most of the families as we pass. Jim Sullivan is shaking his stick, like an irate priest, but it turns out he is only pointing out the black cow that has settled in his road field. Nog acknowledges this, and we keep on.

'We'll take her with us on the way down. She's very close to droppin it. We'll have another birthday.'

The graveyard is down a short lane between two fields. It is set out beside the ruin of an old church, on a slope that looks into the valley. The hill behind affords some protection from the worst weather. This would have been the original settlement in these parts. Down below is a sort of scribbled landscape of wet fields, stone walls and briary ditches with a rise up the far side to the south, and, sure, eventually, if you keep going for thirty miles, there'd be the sea. We walk in through wild grasses studded with grey headstones. Over near a low wall of hairy stones there is a patch that looks like it has seen a scythe or a billhook.

'I came up last week and cleaned it up a tad. There should be an old spade there in along the wall.'

Making myself useful, I go over and find it, a cold, damp inanimate thing. I look to Nog, and he is gesturing towards two rocks that form a crevice.

'If we make a bit of a hole there it should do the trick. What do ye think?'

JJ shrugs his frame.

'That looks like the job.'

I start to root out some weeds and chop into a few sods to create a place. When I start digging brown soil, I get a weird feeling that I am disturbing something different. It's the way the clay is crumbly and dry, despite all the rain.

'She's a well drained site here. That's the way they picked em.'

Nog takes out the tin and is wrapping it in a plastic bag he has brought. JJ is unpacking his sax case and taking out a little tin too. Feck. He hands it to Nog.

'Here, put these in too. I'm not great any more for the comfort and … well, you know …'

I stop digging and lean the spade against the stone wall. I reach into my coat pocket and draw out my own little tin. I offer it to Nog. 'Like I said, set the alarm off at security … better …'

Now we are operating in silence again as Nog is wrapping the three tins together. His head is down, but I can tell he is in difficulty. We all are. I carry on and finish the spadework while JJ clips the sax around his neck. This is it so. The hole is a foot down and neat in against the rocks. Nog looks at us as much to say, who's going to do this. JJ and I gesture to him to get on with it. He kneels down and carefully places the package into the ground. He takes clay between his fingers and sprinkles it down and then stands up with a sigh, or a sob. We copy the business with the clay and then we all stand tight together, heads bowed, and quiet. Once again, nothing needs to be said. Like I said, we've each of us our own prayer.

The evening sun is now sitting down beyond the hill. JJ's sax is a tin-opener on the silence. He is playing the opening bars of the dance tune 'The Hucklebuck'. Mama's favourite. Maybe that's why the father fucked off. The notes swell and fly out from the hillside. Back in the stillness, we shuffle into our own private places. Like three ancient birds, we perch for an age, our feathers tucked in and each possessed of a withered stare.

On the way down, we carefully drive the black cow and see her into the outhouse with the straw bed. We have a meal of corned beef and potatoes and open a bottle of whiskey. I bring out a tube of wasabi paste which I have brought over. JJ grabs it and throws it over to Nog when I try to get it back. They toss it between them, with me as pig in the middle, and it is a bit of gas until Nog tosses it in the fire. That stops the play. There is a long silence in which I try not to sulk. Nog finds a way to apologise. After that the talk is light, like, I suppose, we've almost done enough being brothers ... sons ... for one day. Maybe we are relieved and can start to let our years catch up. JJ glues the head back on the shepherd and spends a while staring into the crib. I sit on the crate over by the fire and start to doze. Nog is at the table with his book.

JJ is first to speak. 'So that's that so. I don't think I'll come next year. It's done. Put me on the headstone.'

'Me too. It's a fair old trek from over the water. And, as you say, it's done.'

Nog closes over his book, and he looks from one of us to the other.

'Did you pair talk about bringin your, you know, tins, together so?'

JJ and myself had not. JJ is looking over at me.

'Well?'

'I've brought mine over with me every year.'

'Me too. Mama – the tin – has always been in my sax case.'

Nog is open-mouthed. 'Well, what the … feckin brillant … what was all that about?'

Indeed, no one had ever said. I'd no idea JJ had done that. All minds working, but not together. Nog is up between us and looking agitated.

JJ again. 'As far as I was concerned it was your move. You had the home ashes somewhere. Not that either of us had any idea where you had them … till today, that is. It was always up to you to make the move. I was happy enough to wait. I was always bringing Mama home.'

'Same as that. Sure we all knew they'd have to go together, sometime, when we were ready. When you were ready.'

'Well, ye pair of feckers, and I was holdin out, I dunno, until today when … ah, feck it, I thought ye'd both lost yours, used them, whatever the feck. I wasn't about to give mine up, but they were startin to freak me out.'

And so it went, back and forward, and back again – sure, we were getting it all off our chests – until the cow called us out to welcome the new boy.

UNDOCUMENTED

MARY MORRISSY

When the invitation to his brother Brian's surprise fiftieth birthday party arrived, Shay was on the afternoon shift in the Maid of Erin on Bergen Street. Once an Irish pub with a definite sense of itself – brown interior, sawdust on the floor, evil-smelling toilets, sing-songs on a Friday night and a clientele of building-site Paddies – 'The Maid' had recently been made over, and, though the inside had been tarted up, the exterior remained the same. The haughty profile of Lady Lavery from the pre-decimal pound note was stencilled across the street window, although most of the current customers, new Irish and gentrified Brooklyn locals who came for the Guinness on tap and the back-room pool table, would probably not have been able to identify who she was.

Although it was a letter from home, Shay didn't recognise the writing because it was from Fiona, Brian's wife. Fee was a frosty-permed control freak, who steered Brian through life with a nifty line in concealed sadism. If there was one thing Shay knew about his eldest brother – and he didn't know much – it was that he hated surprises. But Fee had built a pyramid of them into the fiftieth celebrations: caterers, a marquee, a gathering of seventy friends from various eras of his brother's life and, to top it all, a guest appearance by Shay.

His first response was to throw the invite in the bin and return to work. A lone drinker – one of the old clientele – sat slumped at the bar. Shay took his irritation out on the counter, wiping it down with venom. What was Fee thinking about? He couldn't go home on a whim; Fee should know that. Shay was undocumented, a J1 visa-holder gone rogue, illegal for twelve years. But even when he'd torn the invitation card in two and flung it in the bin, it tantalised him. Was this a way out?

His girlfriend, Petra, had just informed him she was pregnant. She'd stopped taking the pill without telling him. He was furious. Petra was illegal too, so when she'd mentioned children before he'd always said 'not before we get our papers', knowing that was as unlikely as snow in June. He could see the trajectory Petra had in mind: ring on the finger, a house in the 'burbs. That was exactly what Shay wanted to avoid; he'd seen his brothers fall into that trap early – too early. Brian and Dec had gone into the family business, Starling and Sons, the hardware store his father had set up in the forties. His brothers had added two more shops to the original.

'We're expanding the empire!' Brian had said to him, making it sound like the Crusades. 'And you can be part of it.'

A life trading in nuts and bolts, mixing paint and cutting keys; Shay knew he couldn't stand it, and he wouldn't be strong enough to hold out against it. That was why he'd stayed on in New York in August '95, instead of going back for third-year business studies. He'd got as far as Departures at JFK when it came to him, his future all laid out. The family business, keeping the books for Starling and Sons and, in time, marriage, kids and the whole bit. If he was going to bail out, now was the time. So he walked out of the terminal, not even bothering to tell his college mates, and got on the subway back to the city. He felt a surge of power retracing his steps; he was in a place where no one could reach him.

Within weeks he'd found a job serving behind the bar at the Maid, and here he was, twelve years on, a manager. He and Petra had got together at a millennium party in Queens, and their re-lationship had developed in a lazy, unplanned sort of way. She'd moved in because it was cheaper for her, and it meant a cleaner apartment for him. What made it hazardous – and almost like it wasn't really happening – was that it was New York, and he was illegal. It could all disappear overnight in a puff of smoke, so it was a life without consequences. He hadn't counted on Petra ruining it.

'I not put life on hold,' she had declared when she announced she was pregnant, 'just for the papers.' After all these years, Petra had an aversion to verbs, particularly the verb 'to be'. All her conversations had a 'you Tarzan, me Jane' quality.

'Well, you can have it on your own,' he'd snapped at her.

Petra's lower lip wobbled. 'From where you coming?'

'I won't have a gun put to my head,' he said.

'Too late to get rid of it,' she said, stroking the little bump he'd foolishly thought was a charming mid-thirties roundness to her stick-thin figure.

Well, two could play at that game. If he went home for his brother's birthday, that would be it; he couldn't get back. That'd show her! He felt the fiery excitement of an impulse decision. He phoned Fee and said, 'I'll be there!'

The first surprise was at the airport. His middle brother, Dec, came to meet him and had a new woman in tow. She was a real looker – long chestnut hair with a fringe that grazed her eyebrows and a gorgeous figure – supple, sexy – sheathed in a leopard-print blouse and a black spandex miniskirt.

'This is Colette,' Dec said bashfully. 'Meet the baby brother.'

'Hi Shay! Heard a lot about you!' She held out a hand with cherry-red nails.

'And I've heard nothing about you,' he said.

'Yeah,' Dec said proudly.

When Shay had left home, Dec had been married miserably to his childhood sweetheart, Marian. Their mother had died when he was five so Marian was the closest thing to maternal he knew. She'd practically lived with them in the flat over the shop, keeping an eye on all-comers in case Dec might stray. Which was never going to happen. Dec was big, lumbering, soft-hearted and loyal as a kicked dog.

Five years ago, Marian had left Dec. There'd been no children; maybe that had been the problem, though Dec said simply that Marian had gone to 'find herself'. He had come to visit Shay in Brooklyn after the break-up. He got sozzled in the Maid every night, and after Shay closed up he'd pour Dec into bed with promises that there were more fish in the sea. He didn't believe it, though. Who else would have Dec, a forty-two-year-old bloke who smelled of timber and turps, who went to work in a mustard housecoat with the stub of a pencil behind his ear? But Shay had been wrong. This rockabilly chick Colette had nabbed Dec. She sat in the front of the car as they drove away from the airport, swatting her lovely mane over her shoulder and stroking the back of Dec's bludgeoned-looking neck. She couldn't be more than thirty, Shay guessed. Sitting in the back seat, he found himself watching her surreptitiously and thinking … *what the fuck!*

'So, how did you two meet?'

'The shop,' Colette said. 'I came in for thumbtacks and nailed this fella instead.' She smiled indulgently and chucked Dec's cheek. 'No more bad boys for me!'

★

The party was not till the next day, so Shay stayed at Dec's, a three-bed semi he'd shared with Marian. It had a large back garden where the marquee was already being put up. The caterers were arriving with crates of glasses and collapsible furniture. Shay fell into a drugged, jet-lagged slumber in the boxroom. When he awoke in the late afternoon, he hadn't a clue where he was and had to whip back the curtains to ground himself once more – the white-and-blue-striped marquee was now fully erected, and the lovely low golden sun of a suburban summer's evening in Dublin brought him back to himself. He was home.

The next day was all hubbub at Dec's house. Brian's twins, Claire and Amy, arrived to hang bunting and tinsel and, he suspected, to check out their Uncle Shay.

'Dad'll be stoked that you're here,' one of them said.

Shay still couldn't tell them apart. When he'd left, they'd been blonde, pigtailed kids just starting school. Now they were blonde pouty adults, Claire studying medicine in Trinity, Amy 'doing fashion', as she told Shay. They had inherited Brian's looks, grey-eyed, rangy.

'So what's New York like?' Amy asked.

'I manage a bar in Brooklyn,' he told her.

'Cool,' she said, without inflection.

Later, Fee came to supervise the caterers. She brought a stack of large presents for Brian, wrapped in garish paper. She arranged them in a shrine in the living-room picture window. She seemed barely to notice Shay.

'Hi Fee,' he said.

'Oh good,' she said matter-of-factly, 'you got here.' He could see her mentally ticking a box.

There was no sign of the lovely Colette – so she and Dec mustn't live together, Shay thought. He felt, unaccountably, relieved.

Brian's party was set for eight. He had been invited to Dec's, where he thought he was having a cosy birthday dinner, just the four of them – Brian and Fee, Dec and Colette. By seven o'clock, a crowd had gathered in the marquee. A celebratory atmosphere had already built up, thanks to Colette, who circulated with a tray of drinks. She was wearing a dress the colour of an ocean in a travel poster. It was silk, or something very slinky, with a rucked-up bodice and a flowing skirt. Her hair was piled on top of her head in a little bun, and her lips were scarlet. Brian's friends from the golf club, colleagues from the Hardware Association, old school pals, flirted harmlessly with her. Shay recognised some faces from long ago, but no one he could exactly place. Anyway, he was trying to be invisible. Fee had told him to lay low because he was to be the crowning surprise for Brian, but only after the reveal of the party itself and the champagne toast. Shay found himself lurking behind a row of fake box trees that lined the red carpet leading from the French doors into the marquee. At ten past eight, the doorbell chimed in a prearranged pattern.

'That's the birthday boy,' Dec said and left the assembled company in the marquee. Colette took over, putting a finger to her pressed lips, like a pantomime dame. A hush fell. They heard Brian and Fee's voices and Dec sounding falsely hearty. Colette mimed a count of three, and, as the trio of Brian, Fee and Dec reached the French doors, the crowd roared 'Surprise!'

Brian looked like he was going to bolt. He gripped the door jamb and Fee had to prod him forward into the marquee. He was wearing a V-necked jumper like an off-duty priest and a pair of cruelly pressed jeans. (Fee's influence, Shay supposed.) Shay's abiding memory of Brian was of a gangly adolescent, full of first-born certitude and a narrow ambition that went no further than serving behind the counter at Starling Hardware. His motto was 'for the sake of peace'. Don't give Dad cheek, for the sake of peace; don't tell Dad you've failed your exams, for the sake of peace; don't be hard on Dec because … Because Dec isn't that bright is what he meant, though it was never spoken. Brian treated poor Dec as if he were slow-witted. Looking at Colette, Shay thought Dec had outwitted them all. Fee, standing beside her, decked out in white with lots of frills at the hem, looked like a washed-out Bo Peep. Friends crowded around Brian as Fee pushed him deeper into the marquee, and Shay lost sight of Colette. When they were all inside the tent, Fee raised a champagne flute.

'There's one more surprise …' she announced portentously. Brian looked hunted. 'A very special guest has travelled a very long way to be with us tonight.'

She summoned Shay with her crooked finger from his position behind the plastic pot plants. The crowd parted, Red Sea-like, as he presented himself. Brian took one look at him and, to his horror, burst into tears.

'You came home,' he said, sniffling, 'for me!'

The architecture of the Starling family was like an ill-designed playground, the swings and roundabouts of his parents' affections. There were two years between Brian and Dec, then a thirteen-year gap before Shay came along. His two brothers seemed to Shay to belong to an elder ghost family where the spectre of their mother still ruled. Whereas he was like an orphan, a concrete reminder of her late and embarrassing fertility. Now, with his father gone, there was just the three 'boys'. When Dad had died in '99, Shay couldn't come home for the funeral. Not that he and the old man were close, but there were rituals you missed, and burying the dead was one. It seemed to cement his exile. Brian's tears made him think that he had been forgiven.

★

After the toast, Colette sidled up to him. 'Thanks be to Jaysus that's over with,' she said, blowing upwards at her fringe.

'What?'

'All those lies! Planning a surprise party is worse than having an affair. Fee really liked it, though. Maybe she's had some practice?' she said and winked at him as she disappeared into the crowd. The thought of Fee in flagrante delicto made Shay smile.

There were other ritual humiliations in store for Brian. The opening of the presents had to be done in front of everyone, then the first dance with Fee on the duckboards in front of the deejay's stand in the marquee, then a round of 'Happy Birthday' to accompany the cake, which had three tiers and featured a hammer covered in gold leaf. Although it must have been an ordeal, Brian was doing a good job of faking it, Shay thought. He walked among his people, shaking hands like a populist pontiff and being embraced by women dressed to the nines and tottering in heels too high for them. But he didn't come near him. Shay couldn't help feeling that Brian was avoiding him. So much for the biggest surprise of all. He felt more like the prodigal son the fatted calf had forgotten.

There were two portaloos in the back garden, but Shay decided to use the bathroom in the house. It was an excuse to get away from the party, to absent himself. He knew the occasion wasn't about him, but he was beginning to feel like the hired stripper. It was as if, single-handedly, he had brought the party down. After the embarrassing tears, Fee had ordered music to be put on. Amy, the fashionista niece, had a boyfriend who was deejaying for the night and had made compilations of Brian's favourites – Crosby, Stills, Nash & Young, the Beatles, ABBA. Middle-of-the-road shite, in other words. The volume of the nostalgia blasting from the speakers in the marquee, accompanied by the round of smoked-salmon canapés offered by the fleet-footed waiters (obviously drilled by Fee) distracted attention away from Shay, but nobody much wanted to talk to him, and, for the first time, he wondered what the hell he was doing here. He calculated the time difference with New York. Just now Petra would be making lunch (it was a Saturday) – pierogi and sauerkraut – and planning to Skype her parents. Once a week they ate together over the airwaves, a virtual feast.

He tried the bathroom door, but it was occupied. As he idled on the top step of the stairs, he worked out in his head when the baby would be born. His baby. September, he reckoned.

'Penny for them?' Colette stood looking down at him from the bathroom doorway, an amused grin on her face.

'If I tell you, you won't burst into tears?'

'Don't beat yourself up about it. He was thrilled to see you, I'm sure of it.'

'You're absolutely gorgeous,' he said. It was out before he could stop it. Perhaps it was the bubbly and the several glasses of wine he'd had, or Brian's outburst, or just being so suddenly displaced – home, but at sea. Whatever it was, it just popped out of his mouth. In all the years he'd been with Petra, he'd never said anything emotionally spontaneous. She, on the other hand, was always complimenting him, to soften him up, he suspected. She'd sigh about the colour of his eyes, or the cuteness of his arse, his lean looks, his shoulder-length hair, as if she just couldn't help herself. But he'd never felt like that about her. About anybody. In that moment, he felt he'd been pretending forever. Not any more. He leaned in towards Colette. She stepped backwards, and he tripped on the top step of the stairs, and the pair of them fell on top of one another on the swirly carpet on Dec's landing. He looked into her eyes – hazel flecked with amber – and kissed her.

They staggered back into the bathroom, not even bothering to close the door. Her head was crushed between the bowl and the side of the bath. The shower curtain dripped on his hair. While he unzipped, she unbuttoned the top of her dress and pulled up the skirt of it, wrestling furiously with her knickers; he could hear her kicking off her shoes. The recklessness and the sheer strangeness of her excited him. Not a word was spoken. When Petra and he did love (her phrase) there were sweet encouragements – baby, baby, yes, yes … But Colette was different, silent, intense, pliable. At the moment of climax, he fell, triumphant, on top of her. His head crashed into her face.

There was a sickening crunch, and suddenly he was covered in blood. Her nose was pumping profusely.

'Jaysus,' she breathed as if it were an endearment, 'I think you've broken my nose.'

He leapt up and stood over her. Blood seemed to be pouring from her mouth. The top of her turquoise dress was sodden, the maroon stain seeping and creeping across her breasts. She was groaning softly, but he wasn't sure she was even conscious. What the hell was he going to do? His first instinct was to flee. But he couldn't do that, could he? He stumbled down the stairs and made for the marquee. As it happened, there was a break in the music. He raised his hands and noticed they were covered in blood.

'Is there a doctor in the house?' he shouted at the top of his lungs into the silence. Only then did he look down at himself to find more of Colette's blood smeared on his shirt. Brian's daughter Claire, dressed in a pink jumpsuit and a pair of purple stilettos, came towards him.

'I'm a doctor,' she said in a little girl voice, 'sort of.'

Shay had the impression of the party crowd, as of one, moving in behind her, their festive expressions frozen.

'What's happened, Shay?' Brian asked, detaching himself from the crowd. 'What's wrong?'

'It's Colette,' he managed to get out. 'Something's happened to Colette.'

★

It was Dec who sprinted forward, pushing Shay out of the way and running into the house, taking the stairs two at a time. Shay followed in dread, not sure what state of disarray he'd left Colette in. Doctor-in-waiting Claire took up the rear.

Colette was still half-sprawled on the floor, but she'd managed to cover her breasts and pull her underwear up under the dress and was half-sitting up with her back against the bath. There was blood everywhere, great pawmarks (his) on the shower curtain, his smeared footprints on the tiled floor and more pooling in her crushed lap. Could a broken nose produce this much blood? When Colette looked up, she was greenly pallid.

'What the …?' Dec roared, then turned on Shay. 'What did you do to her?'

'He found me, Dec,' Colette said weakly. 'He just found me, that's all.'

Dec knelt down in front of her. Even on his knees he seemed to tower over her.

'I must have fainted,' Colette said, 'and cracked my nose on the way down.'

'I can look at it,' Claire offered half-heartedly, but Dec brushed her out of the way.

'Oh, my poor baby, are you all right?' he crooned at Colette.

Colette looked directly at Shay. They shared a moment of congealed shame before Dec swept her up in his arms, blundered out of the bathroom and into the bedroom at the end of the landing, shouting over his shoulder, 'Someone call 999!'

That was the end of the party. For a while, the revellers sat around in the marquee amidst the wandering balloons, the tables littered with the remains of birthday cake and the froth-smeared glasses. Then, one by one, they made their excuses and melted away until it was just Brian, Fee and the girls, and Shay. They sat in the kitchen, the only room not contaminated by the incident, and drank coffee.

'Why did you really come home?' Brian asked as they sat in the gathering dusk. Nobody bothered to turn on the light.

'You know why,' Shay said. 'Fee asked me.'

'I know that, but you didn't come home for Dad, so why now?'

Shay thought of Petra and blushed in the darkness.

'Didn't you have a girl over there?' Fee said. She had met Petra on one of her outlet shopping sprees to New York.

A girl, a baby, both of them thrown away just to teach Petra a lesson. Shay felt a sudden urge to confess.

'I made a pass at Colette,' he told the gloaming. 'I jumped her in the bathroom …' Once he said it, he wondered if it was true; had she been up for it, or had he forced her? He didn't even know that much any more. 'I mean, we collided …'

'What did you say?' Brian demanded, and stood up. For a

minute Shay thought he was going to strike him. 'You little bastard ...'

'Brian!' Fee said.

'No, Fee,' Brian said. 'No, he's trouble. Always has been. He breaks things. Broke poor Dad's heart, threw his good education back at him. Never finishes anything. Drops people ... too bloody selfish to put his shoulder to the wheel with Dec and myself. All these years we've slaved ... while he's had his precious freedom. He's a bad apple, and that's all there is to it. Condemned out of his own mouth.'

Behind him, Shay could see Claire and Amy, agog at their normally placid father losing the plot.

'Calm down, Brian,' Fee said, making him sit.

Shay peered at Fee, but he couldn't see her expression in the shadows.

'The thing is, Shay,' Fee said evenly, 'you probably don't know, but Colette's pregnant. She's had a couple of those fainting fits, so, you know, we're all worried about the baby ...'

Jesus, is that where all the blood came from?

'But this was an accident. You bumped into her, and she fell,' Fee was persisting, 'or she came over weak, and you tried to save her ... that's what must have happened. You've got confused what with all the panic ...'

He could see how this was going. He couldn't tell the truth without dropping Colette in it. What had gone on between them, their moment – whatever it was – was going to be papered over.

'You're right, Fee … I just feel responsible, you know, finding her like that.'

He could hear Brian exhale. Shay stood up and went to turn the light on. He'd had enough of the half-dark. It was one of those fluorescent bulbs that flickered several times before reaching a buzzing constancy. In the bluish hum he saw Fee staring at him sourly.

'We'll just have to pray the baby's all right,' Fee said.

'And we won't be telling poor Dec about any of this, do you understand?' Brian added, including the girls in the warning.

'No,' Fee said, 'he doesn't deserve that. Now, let's start the clean-up. By the time they get back, it'll be as if none of this has happened.'

Yes, Shay thought, yes. He could call a taxi right now, and, before it was even tomorrow, he could be on the next plane home. Then he remembered. He was home.

GOLDFINCH IN THE SNOW

ÉILÍS NÍ DHUIBHNE

azzlingly, like tropical birds, thousands of reflections floated in the river. Green and yellow and electric blue in the inky water. Flamingo pink. It lifted the heart to see them. 'Lifted' isn't the right word, Darina thought. She knew lots of words; since she'd been in school she'd been making lists of words and phrases and idiomatic expressions and learning them off by heart because that was the path to fluency. Even so, she often couldn't find the word she needed, for lots of things. But, cheer up, it wasn't just English words that failed her; there were things she couldn't find the right word for in her own language, too. The heart leaped up? It jumped, it bounced or maybe what it did was more like what a waterskier does, flying over the waves at high speed with the foam rising around her, like champagne bursting from a bottle, celebrating. Darina had watched them, at Golden Beach, at home, in the harbour below the hotel where she'd worked as a chambermaid. They looked hardly human, the waterskiers. They looked as glamorous and brave and fast as gods. It was hard to believe that some of those superhuman creatures transformed into the holidaymakers whose rooms were left like the wreck of the … what? *Spartacus*? That was a line from the classroom. Those gods were the very same tourists who swayed around the bars of the town in the small hours of the morning.

Pissed out of their heads.

She hadn't picked that idiom up in school, but from Mark, her boyfriend over here. He was to meet her here, outside Tara Street station. He was to have met her, he should have met her, he ought to have met her, twenty minutes ago. The lights down the river sparkled, pink and green and yellow, and the big wheel down at the Point rotated slowly against the sky, and the city looked like magic in the snow, but her feet were feeling the cold. Oh, it was a bitter night, the north wind doth blow, and we shall have snow, and what will poor robin do then, poor thing? Again. Mark was always late, that was an Irish thing, Natasha who worked with her in the café said. Being careless about timekeeping. Darina shouldn't take it personally.

Her phone vibrated against her thigh. He couldn't meet her, she should make it to the party on her own and maybe he'd be there.

Maybe.

What Mark forgot was that the buses didn't run after nine o'clock tonight, New Year's Eve. And Darina had never known that because she didn't listen to the news. Didn't even have a radio. Half an hour later, her feet were really frozen. She was wearing her high heels and her black lacy stockings with the spots, she wanted to look good tonight, she'd high hopes. Of a proposal, actually. If she was honest, and she usually was, she wanted to get married to Mark. Getting engaged wasn't cool, even at home it wasn't cool. But if they got married, she'd belong here. More. A bit more. Plus she really loved him. She loved him so much that she felt he was her other half; when he was away that time during the summer and hadn't got in touch for a week, she felt that she hardly existed. The minute he walked through that door at the airport something snapped back together in her, just like a fastener on a duvet snapping into its hole. She was complete again, everything felt just right. That was the sign, the sign that he was the one for her, her soulmate. Like the sole of her shoe, snapped onto it. Barefoot she'd be, without him, her feet frozen, her heart frozen, the whole country of Ireland a frozen meaningless place.

A taxi.

Such a waste of money – she earned the minimum wage at the café, and now after Christmas it would be down forty euro a week, Natasha had said, or else they'd be sacked, and there were plenty who'd be glad to take their places. They all knew it, the boss and the government and Natasha and Darina. This one taxi ride would cost what she would lose in wages next week. Or nearly.

'About thirty,' he said, nettled, when she asked – Darina always asked, she wasn't one bit Irish in that way, the asking way.

'Okay, it will have to do.' Like an iceberg. She dived into the front seat.

The taxi man gave her one of those sideways looks people gave her often. His head hardly moved, but his eyes slid to the side of their sockets and looked her up and down, from her long black hair with the tiny red cap on top, to the scrap of yellow silk at her throat, to the black spotted stockings. Probably could not see her shoes, black patent, strappy, more sandals than shoes.

'Did anyone ever tell you you shouldn't sit in the front seat?'

They had, but she'd forgotten because she seldom took a taxi in Ireland, because they were such a rip-off. Her room was in the city centre and so was the café. Mark had a room in Trinity, and she met him there. He was at home with his family for Christmas, out in some suburb, where she'd never been; hence the train and all this mess.

'I forgot.'

'No offence, just telling you for next time.' He laughed, and his laugh was a little snort such as some animal might make before it pounces on its dinner. 'Some lads would take it as a come-on, do you know what that means?'

She smiled tightly, and a black arrow nipped her somewhere between the chest and the stomach but she said nothing.

She couldn't see the taxi meter.

'It's broken,' he explained, when she asked. Darina always asked.

'Oh!'

You would think it would be visible anyway. She asked how he would figure out the fare, if he didn't have a meter.

'I'll figure it out, never you fear. It'll be a fair fare,' he laughed, and his laugh was hard and impatient.

Then it was his turn to ask. He asked her where she was from. He asked her how long she'd been over here. He asked her what she worked as. He asked her if there was work in her own country. Then he stopped asking and started preaching. He had nothing against foreigners. They were as entitled to be here as anybody else, the Irish had gone everywhere looking for work so who were they to criticise anybody?

He was all in black, black shirt and black hoody and black jeans, black as a crow. But he smelled nice. That was strange. Some nice soap or aftershave, flowery. There was another undersmell in the car that she couldn't identify, not as pleasant, maybe an apple rotting under the seat. But it was warm in here, so lovely and warm, her toes pained, but in the nicest way, as the life rose back into them like sap in the hyacinth Mark had given her at Christmas.

Then, hey ho, she was running into the sea with her brother. The big high-rise hotels behind, but the blue sea they called the Black Sea in front, the white boats and the white birds, the women in their bikinis, like tropical birds, and out there, far away, the waterskiers, speedy and glamorous and brave as seagulls, with the surf spraying around them. And how curious, because her brother was dead. The black shaft again, piercing. He had been killed in a car crash a few years before she left. She's only dreaming, but why is her bed so hard and so cold?

It's freezing cold, and there's snow on it. He's hurting her – that's not the word, she knows the right word but doesn't say it even in her head, as if not saying it will make it not be happening. She asks him to stop. Darina always asks. But no sound comes out because his hand is over her mouth and the yellow silk scarf has tightened on her throat. In the snow she sees something red glittering, and that is maybe her red cap. Or maybe it is her red blood. The stars glitter in the dark blue sky like sparkling champagne while he works at her as if she were just some machine.

She closes her eyes, though she knows this is not a dream now, not a nightmare. She can't believe it's happening, but she knows. Somehow you do know, always; even while you are in a dream you know somewhere in your bewildered head that it's a dream. After you are six or seven you can tell the difference.

The asphalt is hard and freezing under her thin coat, and her stomach heaves, and then her eyes shut anyway though nobody would ever sleep on a bed as hard and cold as this. Her eyes shut and switch out the light of the stars.

From the dense silence of the frost, a familiar sound.

Shush, shoosh, shush, shoosh.

The shingle scrambles after the sucking surf.

They learnt the line at school, far away from this place, when her brother was alive and when they all still lived at home. It was about that time that she wrote the poem into her copybook, with the line about the surf in it, when she was fourteen and he was fifteen, just before their father taught him how to drive.

Sometimes their sea, the blue sea that is called the Black Sea, takes on a pale, milky colour, where it meets the sky. The sky then too is a pale bluey grey. This happens when the sky is cloudy, at start of the day. She loves the sea best at those times. She loves that colour, which she could never find a word for, maybe because there is no word for it, in her language or in any other. It is just a colour that the water has at certain moments, that reminds her of things she can't name. Pearly, maybe, pearl blue. She was in love with the sea at those moments, more than when it was bright and brash and glamorous, electric in the late morning sunshine when all the tourists of Golden Beach were zipping through it like gods on silver skis.

No One Knows Us Here

Claire Simpson

When the sun dips behind the Botanical Gardens, he unlocks the gardeners' shed and flicks on a light. His heavy gloves are wet and leave a smear on the light switch. Quickly, he separates the blades of his secateurs, wipes them with an oily rag and picks up a fine sharpening stone. He rasps each blade, then tests their edges against his thumb.

Wind rattles the loose window. Tomorrow he will look for any hanging branches that are ready to fall, prune the rest of the trees and make a start on chipping damaged branches into mulch. He checks his phone for the weather forecast, hoping it will stay dry.

'John? Did you not hear me knocking?' His friend Robert walks in and raises two paper coffee cups. 'Got you some rocket fuel.' Robert is only thirty-four but has the hollow, desperate face of a Victorian bushranger headed for the gallows.

'Are you finished?' John says. The younger man smells sour, as if he has worn the same work clothes for a few days.

'I've done enough for today.' Robert hangs up his reflective jacket on a hook, pulls off his muddy boots and throws them into a corner. 'So, are we going out for a beer?'

'I need to stay. Half of the trees in my section are damaged.'

Robert chews on a callous on his thumb; his white teeth worry at it until a chunk of skin peels away. 'Are you getting overtime?'

'There's a lot to do. I haven't even had time to cut up that fallen oak.'

'Come on,' Robert says. 'That place near mine was decent, wasn't it? You didn't seem to hate it too much.'

John feels a muscle twitch in his back. He pushes out his elbows and stretches his arms above his head, but it does not help. 'One drink, okay? I want to come back at seven.'

He puts the secateurs into his toolbox, locks it, then firmly slides the bolt over the shed door.

On the road, the traffic moves slowly. A motorcycle in the inside lane backfires, making them both jump.

'I tried to ring you this morning to see if you wanted a lift but couldn't get through,' John says. 'You still have your mobile, don't you? It hasn't been cut off again?'

Robert flicks on the radio and jabs at the search button until 'Thunderstruck' screeches from the speaker. 'I already told you the phone company made a mistake about my bill that time.'

'Okay, okay.' He notices Robert shivering and turns the heater on full. 'So you're all right for money?'

'Fine.'

John follows the car in front until the turn-off to the coast road. On the seafront, he spots a space close to the pub and pulls into it. In his rear-view mirror, grey waves swell up, fall and slap against the harbour.

'Are you sure this place won't be too busy?' John says, but Robert is already pushing through the double doors.

Coming in from the dark street, the pub feels bright. Strip lights reflect off the brushed metal tables and the yellow flashes on Robert's trainers. Young men, office workers in shirts and undone ties, are shouting at a football match on television.

'We're not serving food tonight,' the barman tells John. 'The chef's gone home sick.'

'Nothing?'

'There's just some curly fries.'

'They'll do.'

John orders two pints and watches the barman draw back the tap and fill each glass. Bubbles filter through the yellow liquid and pop on its surface.

'You're not from here are you?' the barman says.

'No.'

'Anywhere I'd know?'

'It's a small place. Not like here,' John says.

He takes the pints back to their table. The cold beer spills over the lips of the glasses and drips onto his fingers.

'Hey. Don't waste it,' Robert says. 'I'll take mine before you drop them both.'

John allows himself a small mouthful, just enough to swill around his mouth. He sits back in his chair and taps his fingers against each knuckle.

When the barman brings over the fries, they are under-cooked and lukewarm, with a thick crust of salt. John tastes one, then pushes his plate away.

'Do you know, it's my fifteenth anniversary on Friday,' he says.

Robert looks blank.

'At the gardens,' John says.

'Christ, that long? I must be there fourteen years then.'

A fruit machine chatters in a corner close to the bar. The office workers cheer when a goalkeeper kicks away a ball spin-ning towards his net. A clock on the wall ticks past the hour, and John shifts in his seat. He must leave soon.

'Do you remember when I came over and you met me at the airport?' Robert pulls the shiny film off a bar mat and begins to shred the cardboard layers. 'I was thinking about my lost bag. I never did get any compo. Do you think it's too late to chase the airline for it now? They might still have me on the system?'

'Bit late now,' John says.

The match finishes, and the men at the other table call out to the barman to bring them another round.

On television, a woman in a shiny red jacket reads through the news headlines. A missing child, politicians arguing, a crash on the main motorway. John takes another sip of his beer and, when he glances at the screen, sees police leading a man in dirty blue jeans into a marked car. He takes in the man's lined face and his grey hair, the hard set of his mouth and the hands clasped in handcuffs. The man climbs into the car. John feels that if he closes his eyes he will see the imprint of that face on the inside of his eyelids.

There was snow on the ground when the war began. It was November, and he was old for a conscript at the age of thirty-two, sitting in an army lorry on the road to a village he had never heard of. They passed tall poplars tipped with snow and fields where workers were harvesting the last crop of winter cabbages. He shifted his gun and imagined that the past few weeks, tanks moving down his street, his call-up and shooting at empty beer bottles in a football stadium had happened to someone else.

They stopped halfway to the village, and some of the men pissed into bushes by the road, steam rising in the air. Their commander, Marcus, got out of the driver's cab and chatted to the men about basketball. He could have been a professional, he said, and jumped on the spot, pretending to slam dunk a basket beside John.

The rifle was cold and blunt in John's fingers. He looked at Robert and the other men in his unit, all teenagers, all drawing on cigarettes clamped between their thumbs and forefingers.

Too soon, the lorry moved over the brow of a hill towards a cluster of red-roofed houses. Through the plastic window slit he saw a woman throw down her washing basket and run inside a house. Marcus called the order, and John climbed out with the others, the taste of metal in his mouth.

The men dragged people out of houses and made them kneel on the road. Marcus fired the first shot into the papery skin above the neck of a man's blue shirt. Soon the snow was pockmarked with bullets. More men fell. Blood spread and thickened. An old woman collapsed. Robert fired at a teenage boy at the other end of the line. John fired at a man in the middle, then another.

A woman, older than him, began shouting, dragging at his sleeve. John pulled her by the elbow, past where soldiers were piling up dead bodies. A barn door was lying open. He pushed her into the dark and drew a bolt across the door. Straw prickled his knees. He clutched her clumsily, both hands digging into her shoulders. She did not make a sound, not even when the smell of burning bodies filtered into the barn.

When he opened the door, the houses were alight. He stood for a moment, his hand pressed against the wall, when the woman's mobile phone began to ring. The first few bars of a pop song played until he pulled it from under the woman's stomach and smashed his heel against it.

Robert is staring at the television set. His thin lips are the same colour as his face. 'Is that Marcus?' he says.

On the screen, a man's fuzzy outline peers from the police car as it pulls away from a clapboard house. Just in shot is a black dog, jumping and barking behind a wire fence. The car moves down the street, past trees growing too close to overhead power lines.

'I know that road,' Robert says. 'It's only ten minutes away.'

The screen flicks back to the woman in the red jacket.

'Why was he here?' John says. His palms sweat and slip against his pint glass. His stomach contracts, and he swallows. 'Did you know he was living here?'

'What?' Robert says.

'Marcus. Did you ever see him?'

John drains the rest of his pint. The newsreader speaks about threats to the Prime Minister's Immigration Bill, monkeys that escaped from the city zoo and the football match that has just ended.

In the toilet, John runs cold water over his wrists, splashes it on his neck and swallows some of it.

His face is hot, and he wipes it with a paper towel, not wanting to look at his reflection in the mirror above the sink. He feels as if he is recovering from an illness. He imagines police arriving at his house, battering the door down. Or, worse, a squad car turning up at the gardens, officers dragging him handcuffed through the main gates.

When he sits down at his seat again, Robert is still staring at the screen.

'What if they find us through immigration?' Robert says. His right leg jiggles against the underside of the table and almost knocks over an empty glass. 'Why didn't we change our names?'

'Stop,' John says. He hunches forward and covers his cold fries with a napkin. He thinks of coming to this strange country, flying over the sea and a desert that stretched for miles. Why did he choose here? Because there was nowhere further from home.

Robert pulls his chair closer. In the heat of the bar, his sour smell is stronger. 'Do you ever think about those people?'

'What people?'

'In that village.'

'I can't have any feelings about it,' John says. 'It was years ago.' He wipes his finger around the top of his glass.

'Marcus made me fire,' Robert says.

John looks up at the television again. He thinks of the few bars of that song on the woman's phone, how he smashed it before the tune could finish.

'You were conscripted. So was I,' John says.

'We could have said no.'

The other men get up to leave, their laptop bags knocking into each other.

'It will be okay,' John says. 'Do you want another pint?'

'I'm going to go,' Robert says and puts a note on the table.

John crumples the note into his friend's hand. 'I will ring you tomorrow. Nothing is going to happen. No one knows us here.'

'Marcus was here,' Robert says.

John sits in the empty bar, and one beer slides into another. By eight o'clock he is too far gone to drive back to the gardens, so he drinks, and the backs of his eyeballs slowly dry out. Blood spins in his skull. He thinks of how long it has been since he was last drunk, not for years, not since he left home. The fruit machine powers down, and the lights in the bar go out, one by one, until only a bare bulb over the till is shining.

Outside, wind whips the trees on the seafront and the sky is a dark block. He sits on a wet bench and looks at the sea slipping away from the smooth, grey beach. The longer he sits, the easier it will be for him to fall asleep, so he stares down the road at the trams and the headlights of cars and tries not to blink. A gust of wind tugs at his T-shirt, and he lets his head fall back until it touches the back of the bench, slightly spongy from the winter rains and sea spray kicking over the harbour wall. He thinks of the woman and the meaty smell of burning bodies. His eyes close, and he hears the tram pull smoothly away, like a bolt sliding over a door.

CLEANLINESS IS
NEXT TO GODLINESS

DARRAN MCCANN

Terry watched it happen as if in slow motion, but he was too slow to react. By the time he processed what was taking place before his eyes, it had already happened. His daughter Elle dug her little fists into her bowl and threw them up into the air, sending cereal and spilled milk raining in all directions.

'Damnation!' Terry cried. The gloop of lukewarm milk and oats was splattered against his clean white shirt and the pink-and-green stripy tie that Elle had bought him for Father's Day. (Actually his wife Rebecca had bought it for him and signed Elle's name to it. Elle was thirty months old.) Rebecca saw the mess Elle was making and tossed a wet cloth over to Terry.

Terry used it to wipe Elle's hands clean before they could do any more damage. 'I'm late for work. I'll have to change. I can't go into the office spattered in God-knows-what,' Terry said.

Rebecca was at the sink, pouring bleach and scrubbing.

'Can't you feed Elle before you go? I'm late too, and I'm not even dressed yet!' Rebecca protested. It was true. She was still in her pyjamas, and it was after eight. Terry looked imploringly to his son, Michael, who was staring catatonically into his corn-flakes. 'Michael, help me feed your sister would you?' he said.

'Huh?' said Michael.

'Your sister. Help me feed her?'

'I'm, uh, late for school,' Michael said. He looked exhausted. Terry knew to look at him that he'd been up half the night again, playing *Medal of Honor*. Terry held up a spoonful of por-ridge to Elle's face, like an angler hoping his quarry will bite, and Elle regarded the spoon for a moment, then regarded her father, then looked around to her mother, who was still work-ing at the sink. 'What's Mummy doing?' Elle said.

'I'll tell you if you eat a bite of your breakfast,' Terry bargained.

Elle thought about it for a moment, then ate a slurp of cereal and repeated through a full mouth: 'What's Mummy doing?'

'She's cleaning out the sink.'

'What's that?'

Terry looked at what he thought Elle was pointing to. 'It's bleach,' he said.

'Why is it bleach?'

Rebecca looked over her shoulder, and she and Terry ex-changed indulgent smiles. Elle was so sweet when she wanted to know why. The innocence! 'Because it's made of chemicals.

It kills the germs.'

'What's germs?'

'Bacteria.'

'What's ke-teria?'

'Meanies.'

'Meanies are Bad Guys, aren't they?'

'They sure are.'

'Is she killing them all?'

'I hope so.'

'How many?'

'I don't know. Millions.'

'Why is Mummy killing millions?'

'So the sink will be clean.'

'Why?'

'Cleanliness is next to godliness.'

Elle chewed her lip a moment and thought about this. Then she said, 'What's that?' And Terry supposed she meant godliness.

Terry had to admit he wasn't much help in the mornings. His work started earlier than Rebecca's, and he had a commute to contend with, so he tended to worry about getting himself out the door, which meant Rebecca was usually left holding the baby, literally. She didn't mind Terry taking priority, not usually, she understood that Terry had a stressful job and that that job paid the bills and allowed the family to live as well as it did. Rebecca's job, caring for children without parents, paid barely enough to cover the costs of her doing it. 'I need to keep in touch with the workforce,' she often said, always the same slightly metallic tone, always that same exact phrase. Terry wondered where she'd heard it first.

While Terry had been thinking about this, Elle had picked up her spoon and started feeding herself with gusto. Terry loved it when she ate. He drew sustenance from watching her literally draw sustenance, and it had sometimes occurred to him that there was probably something quite poetic about that. When he rose from the table, Rebecca handed him a sandwich wrapped in cling film, an apple and a lunchbox, and he put the sandwich and apple inside the lunchbox. He noticed that Rebecca kept checking the clock, and when he looked at it too, he realised was going to be late. 'Crap,' he said.

He changed into a sky-blue shirt, which complemented his tan chinos rather fetchingly, and went to pick out a clean tie but decided that today he would go open-necked. Why not? You never saw Zuckerberg, Brin, Page, Gates or Jobs, rest his soul, wearing a tie. Nobody with real balls wears a tie any more, he thought. He knew his boss, Adam, would give him a hard time about it, Adam was such a little pedant, but Terry already knew what he was going to say. He was going to say, 'I didn't realise we had a uniform in this office. I must've missed the memo.' That would show him.

When he came back to the kitchen, Elle was wailing in the high chair, and Rebecca seemed stressed. 'Are you okay?' Terry said. When she didn't answer, he said, 'I'd better go.' He kissed Elle, kissed Rebecca too. She seemed annoyed but allowed him a kiss. He wasn't sure what he'd done wrong. He left.

As he drove the thirty minutes to work, the traffic was heavier than usual. Terry noticed people in bright-coloured shirts, families packed into people-carriers, cars with bicycles and even surfboards attached, among the traffic. The weatherman on the radio said it was going to be a scorcher. Terry would have liked to have been going to the beach too, instead of looking at a screen all day. He inched through the traffic and wasn't far from work when he remembered that today was the day Rebecca was interviewing for promotion. He cursed bitterly and took out his mobile phone to call her immediately. Rebecca picked up. Elle was bawling in the background. 'I'm so sorry I forgot about the interview,' he said.

'That's all right,' said Rebecca in her stoic voice. 'I've got to go. I'm driving. I'd better get off the phone before I kill somebody.'

Terry arrived at the airy, pristine new building where he worked, a gleaming cube of glass and natural light. It was a great improvement on the dirty, dark, Byzantine stockade where the department had been based previously. This place was much cleaner. But he'd been under a lot of stress in the office lately. Before, he'd been much freer to make things happen; if he wanted to push a button he could push it. Now he had to get a green light from Adam, and, though Adam never refused, it was still an inconvenience. He was sure it did nothing to help him accomplish the goals he'd been set, and probably hindered him. But the higher-ups were only interested in covering their own asses.

Terry swiped his pass at security, then placed his fingers on the panel. His palms were sweaty with the heat, and, not long ago, this might have prevented the computer from reading his prints properly, but there was no problem any longer because the technology was so much more sophisticated these days. He scanned his retinas, and the door opened. Inside, sitting at the X-ray metal detector, Mick and Herb wore their usual bored expressions. Terry placed his keys, coins and mobile in a tray. 'Morning, guys,' he said.

'Morning, Mr Nelson,' said Mike, the younger and more acutely overweight of the two. 'Glorious day, isn't it?'

'Absolutely,' Terry replied. He noticed Herb hadn't looked up from the screen on which Terry's X-ray scan showed up. He hoped he didn't have a coin in the bottom of his pocket. 'We okay?' he asked, slightly nervously.

'Clean as a whistle,' said Herb.

Terry always tried to be friendly to Mike and Herb, but he always found himself staring at their prodigious waistlines and voluptuous breasts – attributes that identified them as private-sector hirelings. When Terry had started working here, everyone had been public sector, and Terry was fairly certain his own job still was, technically. When they'd first brought in the private contractors, the argument put forward was that the private sector was leaner. But when Terry looked at Mike and Herb, he thought, *They don't look all that lean to me.*

Terry got to his desk in the open-plan office and found a pile of paperwork awaiting him. At a glance there didn't seem to be anything out of the ordinary so he decided to have some coffee before getting started. In the canteen he met Leona, one of the younger staff, who said she was making a cup and would make him one too, if he was interested. 'Two sugars, right?' she said.

'You know me so well,' he replied.

Leona was probably ten years Terry's junior, but as he got closer to forty that seemed less and less like a significant age gap. 'Milky?' she said.

'Black. And scalding.'

'You got it.'

Terry enjoyed flirting with Leona. If he wasn't married he'd have asked her out, and he thought she'd probably say yes. But he had a rule when talking to women: never, ever say anything you wouldn't say in front of Rebecca. He was straying towards the boundaries with Leona, but he had never said anything he couldn't defend. Rebecca wouldn't leave him or anything like that, not over a bit of harmless office frisson.

After coffee, Terry went to Adam's door, which was ajar, and Adam beckoned him inside. Terry said, 'I took a look at last

night's reports. Just a couple of clean-up jobs, nothing unusual.'
He waited for Adam to comment on his lack of a tie, but if
Adam noticed he didn't say anything.

'Fine, fine, that all sounds fine,' Adam replied. He seemed
peeved to be distracted from whatever was on his tablet. 'Oh,
there's a wedding party I want you to look into.'

'Where?'

'One of the usual breeding grounds. It's all in the report.'

'Can I take that as a green light?'

'I trust your judgement,' said Adam.

'That's why you're such a good commanding officer,' Terry
said sweetly, and Adam smiled back viciously.

The day passed. Terry sloughed through briefing documents
on his desk, ticking this box and exing that one. When he
looked out the window, he could see the haze rising on the
tarmac of the car park, and he thought, *Thank God for the air con.*
The paperwork was stultifyingly dry stuff so he went into the
conference room with its twenty large screens. He liked to call
this room the Eye in the Sky, but hadn't managed to make the
name catch on yet. On the screens were grainy aerial pictures of
various sites, and Terry took a seat at the back of the room, behind the banks of desks at which staff were watching the screens
carefully. He spotted Leona at desk six and sidled over to her.

'What are you looking at?' he said.

'The so-called wedding party,' Leona replied.

'How many eyes do we have in that area right now?'

'Four.'

'What's your gut telling you?'

'Intelligence isn't convinced.'

'Intelligence isn't everything. Let's keep an open mind. We have to be extremely judicious,' he said.

Leona looked at him like he was Solomon. He thought, *If I weren't married …*

'But be ready to move when I give the word,' he added. He didn't want her to think he lacked the moral courage to give the order.

'Doesn't Adam have to give the green light?'

'Don't worry about Adam. Just keep watching and wait for my order,' said Terry.

Adam: the snivelling little shit was five years Terry's junior both in age and experience but had leapfrogged ahead because of a well-connected uncle. Terry had got to his position without help from anyone. He knew that sooner or later Adam would screw up, because he had been promoted way ahead of his readiness. And when he did, Terry would move seamlessly into his office. Unless there was another snivelling little shit with a bigshot uncle. And there was always another snivelling little shit with a big-shot uncle. Terry wished he had a big-shot uncle.

Terry checked back later in the day, rubbing an apple against his shirt as he bowled towards Leona, who said she'd noticed some suspicious-looking activity on her monitor. There seemed to be a couple of figures standing forty or fifty metres apart from the rest of the crowd. 'Some wedding party,' Leona said. 'Why would anyone even want to get married in an area that's swarming with bad guys? Who do they think they're kidding?'

Terry leaned in over her desk, looking closely at the monitor. He could smell her perfume. It was cheap and pungent, the sort of stuff Rebecca would never wear. It turned him on. 'Take me closer,' he said.

'If we go too close, the payload could damage the hardware.'

Good, thought Terry. Adam won't like having to answer to his superiors for that. Of course, Terry would have to answer to Adam, but it would be worth it. 'Closer. Go closer. I want to get a good look at these guys. We have to be so very scrupulous,' Terry said.

Leona complied.

'Even closer.' Terry went further. He wanted to be like a giant wasp buzzing around their heads. Leona flew in as low as she could but the figures below were still dots. Terry watched them scurrying around. They looked like germs under a microscope.

'If they aren't doing anything wrong, why would they be running?' said Terry, mainly to himself.

'That's what I thought.'

'All right. Clean them out.'

'Don't I have to clear that with Adam?'

'Let me worry about him. They're getting away. Do it. Clean them out.'

'Yes sir,' Leona grinned, and snapped a childish salute. She tapped her keyboard, and a something projected from offscreen into the centre of the picture. Then the screen went white. 'Shit. I think it's busted,' said Leona.

'We have three more in the area. Nothing to worry about. Get me some estimates on how many bad guys we got. Then you can call it a day.'

'Sure thing boss,' said Leona, her eyes twinkling.

Boss. *I like the sound of that*, thought Terry. He took a bite out of his apple as he swaggered out of the conference room. He was just finishing the apple when, a few moments later, Leona appeared at his desk and said, 'Twenty-four males of military-service age, that's confirmed.'

'That was quick.'

'The all-seeing eye-in-the-sky.'

'Collateral?'

'Still working on estimates. But I think it was pretty clean.'

'Cleanliness is next to godliness.'

Terry knocked again at Adam's door. Adam was still engrossed in his tablet. 'Hope I'm not interrupting?' said Terry.

'What is it?'

'Two things. One, I need to leave a little early on Friday. We're heading away for the weekend.'

'That's fine. What else?'

'The wedding party. Just confirmed. It was no wedding party. We cleaned out twenty-four bad guys.'

'Good, good,' said Adam, still not looking up from his tablet. 'Just put it all in the report.'

'But we may have lost a piece of hardware.'

At last Adam looked up. 'Oh, for Christ's sake!' he exploded. Terry had to fight a smirk. Adam at last put down the tablet, and Terry saw it lying on the desk. He'd been playing online poker.

Terry stopped off for flowers on his way home, and Rebecca gave him an embattled smile when he handed them over. 'How was work today?' she asked.

'Same old, same old,' he said. 'But never mind me! Today is all about you! How'd it go?'

'Okay, I think. I mean, I know I nailed all the questions they asked, and I know I'm qualified. Fingers crossed, I guess.'

'They'd be crazy to even consider anybody else,' said Terry. 'Listen, I'm really sorry I forgot about it this morning. It wasn't good enough. I should have remembered. I know this was a big deal for you. It's a big deal for all of us. I'm a hundred per cent behind you. I bet you knocked 'em dead.'

'Thanks,' said Rebecca, and Terry could tell she appreciated his words.

'I'm really proud of you. You know that, don't you?'

'I know,' said Rebecca. 'Thanks for saying sorry. You're always so good to admit when you're wrong.'

Terry considered the compliment his wife had paid him, and he felt good to think it was true. He remembered reading at college that one of the philosophers had said the unexamined life was not worth living, and he had tried to live by that quote. It was important to step out of yourself and to empathise with others. His wife had needed his support, and he'd been too wrapped up in his own thing to remember to give it. He felt a pang of shame, but it was tempered with a sense that he knew he'd been wrong, and there was virtue in that. He gave Rebecca a big, wet kiss that made her laugh, then gave his daughter Elle a big slobbery smacker too, and crouched down beside his son Michael, who was engrossed in *Medal of Honor*, and laid one on him as well.

'Ahhhh, get off! Gross!' cried Michael, and they all laughed.

After dinner, Terry watched some TV – first the news, then a documentary about the Nazis – before shuffling off to bed. He thought he might read for a while but found he was too tired. He fell into a deep and peaceful sleep within seconds and never stirred till his alarm went off the next morning, calling him to rise for another day's work.

CHARCOAL AND LEMONGRASS

RUTH QUINLAN

He hears the woman rummaging on the thatched veranda. She doesn't interrupt him, just leaves another gift of food under an upturned basket before padding away through the bamboo forest. Until she arrived, the American hadn't realised how long he'd been working.

His joints click as he straightens from his kneeling position on the floor and the old wound in his leg flares into a familiar ache. When he reaches up to wipe the sweat from his forehead, he notices the charcoal on his hands. There are thick black crescents under each fingernail and soot fills every crease. He scrubs them in a basin of water, the scrap of soap turning a darker shade of stippled grey.

Outside, he lifts the basket to find a small mound of *banh chung* – parcels of sticky rice, mung beans, lemongrass and pork wrapped in banana leaves. It is Tet again, when the local women boil stacks of the parcels in their largest pots, sending clouds of steam billowing from stilt-house windows. He piles the *banh chung* into the basket and carries them inside. One he reserves for the kitchen gods and places it as an offering on a tiny altar strewn with orchids and the charred, powdery remains of burned joss sticks. Then he sits cross-legged on the floor and carefully unties the bamboo-fibre bindings on another parcel. He blows on the stuffing to cool it and eats it with his fingers. As he eats, he realises that this is his solitary celebration of yet another new year. Time is passing.

Billy Larsen was born on a farm of golden cornfields, the kind of place with a rusting pickup out front and a lazy creek out back. He grew up working side by side with his father, husking crops of corn and sorghum and tending their herd of calving cows. Like the other young men, he drank beer to a soundtrack of rock and blues, hunted raccoons with his father's rifle and chased girls, pinning them behind the cornstacks and kissing their soft, bubblegum mouths. Unlike the others, however, Billy dreamed of things beyond the placid rhythms of a Minnesota homestead.

Billy's father was one of the few that had survived Omaha Beach. A reserved man, Larsen only spoke about his war after one too many bourbons on the porch. Billy would sit listening at his feet, enthralled as the fields of swaying corn were replaced by the Normandy cliff-tops. The Larsens were the only people not surprised when he enlisted in '63 – just one week after watching a president die in Texas. On the day Billy left for boot camp, his father shook his hand and wished him luck, before turning away, muttering about fixing the barn door. His mother sobbed silently into a tea towel in the kitchen.

Three months later, as the transport Chinooks thrummed above the rainforests towards the field base, Billy was redefining his understanding of the colour green. In comparison to the amber-gold hues of the Midwest breadbasket, Vietnam presented a luxuriant palette of limes, olives, jades and emeralds. The riot of growth was unlike anything he had ever seen, alien and fascinating in comparison to the tidy, geometric shapes of nature that he knew. In the jungle, the other marines cursed and sweated, swatting futilely at the creatures that crawled and bit and stung. Billy adjusted quicker than most, and, with his small build and dark colouring, rumours began to circulate that he had 'gook blood' in him. He laughed it off, yelling across the mess table that he was 'just as American as any other shitbird in the fucking platoon'. But at night, rolled up in his poncho, he wondered why a place the other grunts had christened Hell on Earth felt like where he belonged. For him, the breath of the jungle was like the smell of the cornstacks back home – dark and fertile – and with the churring of the insects, it lulled him to sleep while the other men tossed and turned.

Several months into Billy's tour, on what was supposed to be a routine patrol, heavy Viet Cong fire separated him from the rest of his platoon. Mortar rounds echoed off the surrounding hills, making it almost impossible for him to locate a point of origin. Briefings that week had indicated the discovery of tunnels in the area, and he kept a close eye on the ground. Just the day before, Billy had watched two medics stretcher a bellowing marine into the field hospital, his foot swathed in saturated bandages. The marine had stepped on a hidden trigger, and a trap had fired a bullet straight out of the ground, taking three of his toes with it. 'Toe-poppers' were swiftly added to grunt lexicon.

As he searched for a vantage point on higher ground, the jungle started to thin out around him, the vine-webbed mangrove and banana trees giving way to soaring giants. Abruptly, a clearing surrounded by silvery tualang trees opened out in front of him. In the centre of the clearing, a woman was suspended from a high branch, a rope tied around one ankle and her hands bound behind her back. Her long, black hair hung loose, brushing the leaf-covered ground. A shaft of sunlight had broken through the forest ceiling to illuminate scatterings of pink and white orchids on the barks of the trees behind her. Billy stopped, transfixed by the unexpected beauty of the scene. The cloying perfume of the flowers swirled around him, and he had to lean against one of the low branches, more to ensure he was still awake than to steady himself.

As if she had felt the touch upon her skin, the woman instantly moved to swing around towards him, craning her neck over her shoulder. Relief flickered across her face as soon as she saw him. She started whispering urgently in Vietnamese, gesturing repeatedly with her head towards the north. He caught just one phrase that he recognised – *nguoi linh*. Soldiers. It could have been the local VC that had trussed her up like this, he thought; he had heard of women being dragged off by guerrilla units as they threaded through the jungles. However, there were also stories of servicemen who found even the opium-clouded brothels in Saigon too public for more vicious appetites. He didn't like either alternative.

The rapid stream of foreign words halted, and, gathering her breath, the woman forced out just one, over and over. Billy realised she was trying to say, 'Please.' The simple plea decided him. He unstrapped his knife and reached up to saw through the rope at her ankle. When it split under her weight, she fell heavily to the ground, and he cursed himself for not having freed her hands first. She rolled onto her side and tried to push herself to her feet, but her right leg buckled beneath her. A whimper of pain escaped before she bit down hard on her lip.

'Wait, wait. Just stay still for a minute – I want to help,' he said, trying the same steady tone he had used with skittish animals back home.

She paused and watched him intently as he pointed with his knife, first towards her hands and then towards her ankle. Slowly, she nodded and lay still as he leaned down to cut through the knotted ligature around her leg. Then she mutely held out her bound hands. Billy had to force them apart so that he could ease the knife between them, and, as he did so, he saw that the rope had left deep red weals in the pale skin of her inner wrists.

Straightening up, he took her arm and hauled her to her feet. She took a few hesitant steps, favouring her right leg but managing to stay upright this time. He watched as she made a careful circumference of the clearing. Dead tree orchids were tangled in her hair from the fall, and, as she passed, he had to stop himself from reaching out to pluck them free.

Suddenly she froze, her head cocked towards the south. Billy realised that the pounding of the mortar rounds had moved closer. The woman turned to Billy and bowed solemnly to him before moving towards the tall elephant grass at the edge of the clearing. He started to follow her, but she stopped and held up the palm of her hand, the gesture warning him away. Reluctantly, he stayed, watching the tops of the grass stalks shiver as she passed until he could no longer tell whether the grass moved because of her or the breeze.

He resumed his own path up the hills and had to work hard to force a way through the dense grasses. Sharp edges lashed at his face, and his vision blurred as a mixture of blood and sweat trickled into his eyes. Too late, he noticed that the patch of ground in front of him was oddly bare. The earth gave way, and his right foot plunged downwards. He screamed as something razor-sharp sliced up along both sides of his leg. Desperately, he tried to brace himself as his weight dragged him further into the hole, and he pitched forward, almost bending his knee backwards and sending another burst of agony rocketing up his spine. Training had kept his rifle in his hands, and he grasped it, pushing against the butt to leverage himself off the ground. He balanced as much of his weight as possible onto his left knee and then, after taking a few shaky breaths, leaned over to look into the hole. Inside, he saw two sharpened lengths of bamboo wedged horizontally to point towards the centre. When his foot had broken through the cover, the bamboo spikes had torn into his calf muscle and slashed two deep lines up to where they had hooked on the knee joint. Blood was pouring from the open wounds, and he almost fainted when he saw a white glimpse of bone through the lacerated tissue.

Each time he tried to pull his leg free from the spikes, pain ripped through him, and he came close to passing out. The prospect of lying unconscious and bleeding out into the hole terrified him, and he had to work hard not to spiral into panic. With difficulty, he forced himself to focus on just one small task at a time. He unbuckled his belt and fastened it above his knee, cinching the leather tight in a makeshift tourniquet. The flow of blood started to slow. He shrugged off his heavy pack and set it on the ground next to him. Next, he broke out the magazine in his rifle. Fifteen rounds – and he had another two twenty-round clips in the bandolier. It would have to be enough. He reinserted the magazine, clicked the rifle to automatic and leaned it against the pack, within easy reach. Then, for the first time since he turned eighteen and his mother gave up dragging him to the First Trinity Lutheran church, he prayed.

Gunfire lower down in the valley gradually became more intermittent, and then stopped altogether. The tropical dusk was falling rapidly. He watched the sky striate with pink and mauve, then grey, the interlaced tualang branches high above him etched in black against it. It reminded him of charcoal drawings he had seen hanging from a rickety stall outside Da Nang, shortly after he had first arrived. The monochrome stark-ness of the drawings had arrested him, and he had considered haggling with the aged stall-owner for one. But it had been close to curfew that evening, and he had hurried on. When he went back the next day, the stall had disappeared.

He drained the last of the water from his canteen and leaned over to check his leg again before the light faded. It had gone partially numb. The skin below the belt was white, but he dared not loosen the tourniquet – he wasn't sure he could handle the torture of circulation returning to his mangled limb. Nauseous and cold, he knew that shock was setting in. If he didn't get out of the hole soon, he would die there like a stuck pig. He grabbed a nearby stick and set it between his teeth, then gripped his rifle and lowered it into the hole. Biting down hard on the stick, he began to hammer the rifle butt against one of the spikes, trying to force the point downwards, out of his leg. But he had forgotten that the spikes would be slippery, coated with layers of his blood, and on the next downward thrust, the rifle slipped and rammed into the open wound. The stick in his mouth shattered.

He threw the rifle to the ground and curled himself over his folded left knee, his right leg still embedded in the trap. He tried not to think about eating a bullet, but his brain kept circling back to it, and he knew that the more time passed, the less likely it was that he would even be capable of making that choice.

The grass rustled nearby, but Billy was too spent to even raise his head. It was the VC, he thought, finally come to see what all the shouting was about, and he just didn't care any more. Anything was better than dying in the hole. Two small feet walked into his line of vision and stopped in front of him. He looked up and saw the young woman from the clearing leaning over him, her hair falling in a black curtain through which he could see slivers of the rising moon. She knelt down next to him and laid her hand briefly on his head – a silent benediction.

After a furtive glance at the surroundings, the woman began to dig around the sides of the trap with her hands. She had almost reached the level of the spikes when Billy heard a faint, metallic click nearby. She heard it too and dug faster, sweat creating runnels in the dirt on her face and arms. After a few more seconds, she paused, her eyes meeting Billy's. Understanding what she was about to do, he nodded. She reached down and swiftly wrenched one of the spikes from his leg. In vain, he attempted not to scream, but the pain tore his mouth open. A shot rang out, and the woman lurched forward, Billy instinctively catching her in his arms as she fell. Her hair fanned out across her face, and, when he brushed it away, he saw the bloody crater where the bullet had smashed through her cheekbone. One remaining brown eye stared serenely up at him, perfect except for a tiny, red spray of burst capillaries radiating from the inner corner.

'No, no, no!' he shouted, over and over until he was punched, hard, on the jaw.

'Holy fuck, Private, will you quit the goddamn hollerin',' came a southern drawl almost right next to his ear. A heavily camouflaged marine emerged from the grasses near Billy. 'You want every VC unit in the area down on top of us? Last time, I swear on the Almighty, this is the last time I'm comin' out here, savin' the ass of some shit-for-brains grunt who goes and gets himself fuckin' lost in the middle of a goddamn shoot-out.'

The Texan dragged the woman off Billy and dumped her body over to one side. Taking a deep breath, he hawked up a wad of phlegm and spat it at her. 'Torturin' little fuck.'

Billy didn't even hear the marine, he was so intent on trying to heave himself out of the hole towards the woman. She had tried to repay her debt to him. And now she lay splayed on the ground, with spit drying onto her back and her blood trickling into the hole, mingling with his. Billy gritted his teeth, pulling harder and harder against the spike that still tethered him to the trap.

'You're gonna ruin what's left of that leg,' said the Texan calmly, watching Billy struggle to crawl free. 'Son, you're just gonna have to remember later that I did this for your own good.' With one deft movement, he rotated the muzzle away from him and hit Billy just below the temple with his rifle. Billy collapsed, almost welcoming the darkness.

Sitting alone on the bare floor, the American surveys his handiwork and eats the last of the *banh chung*. As he chews, the taste of lemongrass floods his tongue. Sometimes he misses the food from back home – burgers and fries, malts and cherry pies – but not often.

Here, he is known simply as 'the American', treated as an eccentric by the villagers now that the war is over. The name Billy Larsen belongs to the life he gave up in Minnesota, a life he abandoned when he realised that he would find no peace until he returned, however many blonde, blue-eyed girls he married. A blood pact had been soaked into the earth of the jungle, and it reached out across the seas to hold him to it.

One of the local women lives with him, quietly devoted to the strange foreigner. She is damaged in her own way, unable to bear children since Agent Orange wrapped poisonous fingers around her womb. She brings food to his hideaway in the nearby forest but never asks him what he does there; she is content enough that he provides her with money to run their house in the village and that he offers an odd, distant type of affection. He has never told her that the reason he shares her bed is because she resembles a dead woman. The villagers gossip, saying he is haunted by a Vietnamese girl he fell in love with during the war. He smiles, as they are only half right. He is tormented by the image of a single perfect eye – he sees it every time he closes his own.

He threw away most of the furniture in the hut and ripped out the cupboards and shelves. With everything removed, there was more wall space than he had expected, and it took him several days to coat the walls with those first layers of whitewash.

He brushes the crumbs from his fingers and kneels down again beside the wall. The stick of charcoal is where he left it on the floor. He picks it up and begins to draw again, scratching line after black line into the whitewash. Three of the walls are already completely covered with images of a beautiful woman, her dark hair hanging loose around her shoulders. There is always something wrong about the left side of her face – an imbalance, an uncertainty in the lines that makes her appear unfinished. He knows this, and it drives him on, for he will not stop until he has recreated her exact likeness.

The walls have been whitewashed many times into fresh canvases. But, no matter how hard he tries, he will never complete his task – because Billy has forgotten what the woman looked like before the bullet.

COUNTRY FEEDBACK

MIKE MCCORMACK

It must have looked like a crack in the earth. From the air that is, looking down on it: a great white crack in the earth.

It was early afternoon, just coming up to the lunch time, and I had nearly the whole pool scooped, two hours going through it with a landing net. It's an easy job, and, to tell the truth, there's something soothing about wading through four or five feet of water, something good about having to slow down and make sure you've got your footing solid under your feet.

And it was a nice day working outside. Low, grey skies but no breeze or sign of rain. The rooks in the trees along the bank were raising a ruckus, the sky black with them coming and going. On a quiet day, you wouldn't believe the noise those fuckers can make. Anyway, I was wired up to my iPod so I did not hear much of anything.

It was lucky I saw it coming. If that swell took you by surprise there's only one way you're going to go and that's head first into the water. And it's dangerous falling over in a river with full waders on you. Current suction can drag you down and hold you there.

And I didn't hear a sound either even though the crash must have been loud on such a still day. A lorry that big tipping off the road; it would have made some bang.

I was facing upstream when I saw it coming towards me along that smooth stretch of water above the pool – this wave, about three feet high. I knew I wouldn't have time to make it to the bank so I just turned my back to it and planted the landing net as hard as I could into the gravel and leaned onto it so that when the wave hit me I would be well braced.

Even so, it was as much as I could do to hold my footing. The water surged under me and lifted me forward, both feet leaving the ground for an instant before the wave pushed past and began to level out towards the wider shores of the pond. It took me a couple of moments to steady myself and turn around into the current – was there another wave coming towards me? But no, there were no more waves; that was the only one. It took me a moment to steady myself, and I was just about to make my way to the shore when the water around me began to change colour – the whole river turning white up as far as the bend.

And as I stood there with the water whitening around me I knew we were fucked.

If it mixes with water, milk is more dangerous than oil.

You have some chance with oil — it's lighter than water so it floats and pools. But milk is a bastard. It spreads through the water, down through all the levels, and it chokes off all the oxygen, and if enough of it gets into a river system and that same river system runs through a hatchery, then you're looking at a serious fish kill.

I didn't make it to the lock gate in time.

The water flooded through for about two minutes, and that was more than enough time to kill a whole lot of fry in the holding tanks. When I got there, they were lying belly-up in the milky water, and by the time I got them flushed out, which took twenty minutes, over eighty per cent of the stock was gone.

They were lying on their backs with their gills already whitening.

Three years' work gone in five minutes.

Out in the river, milk was still pouring into the pool from upstream. I stood there for ten minutes looking at it — the colour deepening out towards the bank.

I looked up at the sky and imagined myself looking down from it; that grey fucking sky. And that's when I thought it must have looked like a crack in the earth.

For a split second I could see the shock and disappointment in Eibhlín's face and then that twisting effort it took to bury her disappointment and put a brave face on it.

'It's only fish,' she said.

'It's a disaster, Eibhlín.'

'It could be worse.'

'How could it be worse?'

She raised her phone into the air. 'I got word; Emily Crayn called me. She said there'd been an accident. Thomas Ryan came off the road with the milk lorry – he's been rushed to hospital and he's not well; that's how it could be worse.'

It surprised me to realise that I had not given any thought whatsoever to where the milk had come from. My panicked attempt to save as much of the stock as possible had totally wiped from my mind the most unlikely element of the whole incident – how a large freshwater pool had suddenly filled up with milk and how I had known for certain it was milk from the moment the water turned white around me.

'And that's how it could be worse,' Eibhlín repeated as she laid her lips on my forehead. 'You could be in intensive care like Thomas with pipes leading out of you right now.'

'That bad?'

'So Emily was saying; his family have been called over.'

Eibhlín sat onto my knee and lowered her head onto mine. She smelt of stale perfume and sweat, and I found it arousing as I knew she knew I would. 'So today is not a day to complain – today is a day to count your blessings. Are you playing tonight?'

'Yes.'

'We have a couple of hours so, we could go to bed and count our blessings together.' She ran her hands through my hair, lifting up a great swodge of it.

I patted her arse and turned her towards me. 'All right, let's do that; up those stairs woman, and let's count our blessings.'

So she did and we did.

When I woke, she was sitting on the side of the bed with the works spread out on the side table: vial, syringe and antiseptic wipes. She was swabbing the roll of fat below her belly button.

'Can I do anything?' I asked even though I already knew the answer.

'No, there's nothing you can do,' she said, as she took up the syringe.

So now I'm midway through my set, and the call is for Alan Jackson's 'Remember When'. I like the song; it's just finely balanced between mawk and genuine sorrow, a song you can properly feel your way into. There's two or three couples on the floor, waltzing. They've broken away from the press of people around the bar, and just having these few couples dancing gives the song an extra depth, an extra bit of meaning. I wind it down, and the couples break and raise their hands in applause before they make their way back to their seats.

I lean the guitar against the amp and go to the bar. Helen spots me and passes a pint over the heads of people crushed around me. A Friday night in a small Mayo village; you could be in worse places and you could be in better ones.

There's talk of the crash – the milk truck going off the road is big news. There's a lot of concern and wonder also because Thomas is local and he's been driving these roads for years with the truck.

'I hear he's not good,' a voice beside me says.

'He's in intensive care – the family was sent for. Does anyone know what happened?'

'Marcus Conway was there – he said that the road gave way under the wheels as it was coming into the bridge, and it slewed away over the side.'

'There's a good drop from that road.'

'About thirty feet.'

'That and more.'

'It's not so much the drop as the rocky slope beneath – that's what ripped the tank open. I saw the truck going over the road this evening on the back of Jimmy Lally's low-loader, and you could see the tank was ripped open like a crisp packet.'

So I hear the talk and leave them to it. Back on the small stage for the second part of the set, I lift the tempo for the last forty-five minutes. A couple of Elvis songs – 'Teddy Bear' and 'Jailhouse Rock' – and a couple of Johnny Cash songs – 'Forty Shades of Green' among them – and round it out with 'Friends in Low Places' ... And of course I top the whole thing off with 'The Soldier's Song' ...

And it's been a good night – a nice crowd with a lively buzz and a few couples taking the floor, waltzing and jiving and making the job worthwhile. I lean the guitar against the amp and leave it there; I will pick it up tomorrow afternoon when it's quiet. At the bar, Helen has an envelope in her hand, and she presses it into my hand with a smile.

'Good work, Jamie, you were flying up there. We'll see you next week.'

'See you then.'

The envelope is buttoned into my shirt pocket as I make my way through the crowd and head out into the night.

Eibhlín's in bed when I get home. No lights on except for the digital display on the oven. I toe off my boots beside the range and fill a glass of water from the tap. We have a ritual, and I like to see it observed.

I sit on the bed beside her and roll a smoke in the light pouring in from the hallway; when it's licked and tipped, I lay it on the bedside locker. Then I pull open the drawer and take out the two blister packs and the small jar. I press one pill from each pack into my hand and two from the jar. The popping sound wakes her, and she pushes herself up sleepily against the headboard. With her eyes closed she reaches her hand out, and I place the glass of water in it. One by one she takes the pills, washing them down with a mouthful of water and setting the glass down on the locker.

My acoustic guitar is standing against the wall.

'So tell me about it,' she murmurs, without opening her eyes.

'There was a crowd.'

'Good, anyone dancing?'

'Yes, a few people dancing.'

'Nothing rowdy?'

'Everyone was well behaved.'

'And you got paid.'

'I have it here.'

'Good.'

Her voice murmurs from the edge of sleep. I pick a few strings. 'So what will it be tonight? What do you want to hear?'

'Something soothing,' she says, twisting herself down beneath the quilt, 'something to return me to sleep.'

'How about, "She Ain't Going Nowhere".'

'Okay, "She Ain't Going Nowhere".'

So 'She Ain't Going Nowhere' it is, and she drifts off in the final, fading chorus. Or so I think; just as I'm about to pull the door behind me, I hear her sob.

'Milk,' she chokes softly, 'of all the damn things.'

I light up at the kitchen table but leave the light off. One strange day gone by. Out there in the darkness there is a man in intensive care with his family gathered around him; who knows what the morning will bring them. Up the river there are two large holding tanks filled with dead fish – clearing them out will be tomorrow's work. And down the hall a woman has just sobbed herself to sleep, choked back another disappointment, another setback: one more day of putting a brave face on things. Outside, the night is settling into its full depth, a night flattened over a world drowned in milk.

The clear light of day in which things might look better is a full six hours away.

CELESTIAL ORBIT

BRIDGET SPROULS

Trevor let the bag of textbooks slip from his shoulder and onto the floor with an enormous thud. Downstairs, the neighbour bawled his usual threat, and Trevor's sister laughed because she had never heard it. The onset of adulthood had chipped her front tooth in half, making her smile like a pumpkin. Adults freeze up as they get older and start to look weird, Trevor thought, like camera-shy people or old surprised puppets.

'Your sister's come to stay with us,' his mother said. 'If you're lucky, she'll give you a painting lesson.'

'Right,' Celeste said. 'Totally.' She took a beer from the fridge, twisted off the cap and flicked it wide, into the living room. His mother never bought beer. 'What grade you in now?'

'Ninth.'

Trevor thought his sister looked as though she had just rolled out of bed. She's probably been travelling all day. One brown hem of her jeans was dragging on the floor like a mangy tail.

After dinner, Celeste came into his room. She had showered and now swam in her mother's denim.

'I'm gonna go meet Vicki and some other people,' she said. 'You remember Vicki, right?' Trevor did not remember Vicki, but his sister had never wanted him anywhere near her friends. She was eight years his elder. 'Wanna come? Mom's fine with it.'

He followed Celeste across the empty boulevard to the ocean block. They trudged over the dune and beyond the throw of street lights. Everything was dark. A cold breeze was blowing. Finally Celeste spotted a flock of lit cigarettes.

Trevor's eyes adjusted to the black enough for him to pick out a loose huddle of people.

They sat down among them.

'I brought my little brother,' she said.

Trevor crouched behind her on the sand, partially out of the wind.

'Who's got my candy?' she said, and he thought of the liquorice in the kitchen pantry at home and the butterscotch suckers in the scallop-shaped dish on the coffee table, and he looked with forced intentness towards the ocean, tumbling out of the dark into lines of hissing grey.

Celeste and someone else got up and smacked away the sand.

'Stick around,' she said. 'I'll be back.'

He wondered why she had asked him to come.

Trevor listened to the other three shapes' varied complaints; my life may depend on it, he thought, then wondered at the childishness of it.

'I got work at the ass crack of dawn,' said a woman's voice.

'Let me call you Dawn,' said a man.

The woman squealed in surprise, then her voice dropped to a whimper. Trevor looked towards the huddle after a silence. He saw only two shadows, now flat against the sand, one on top of the other in a dark grey sandwich. Wet heat travelled the back of his neck. He tingled everywhere, and his sleeping thing woke up.

Get away, he thought. The tongue went in his ear. Why not let this happen? A hand gripped him. It might be important … No, it's weird. Make it stop. Hurry. But, clutching a handful of sand, no no no, he lost control. Get away, he remembered and ran through the dark.

His mother heard him come up the stairs and called him over to sit with her in front of the TV. He wished he could take a shower, but she would think it peculiar. He normally showered in the morning.

'I'm tired. G'nite.'

'Where's your sister?'

'Out.'

'You came back alone?'

'It was boring.'

'What was boring?'

'Jesus, Mom! You want me to spy on her or something? Who cares.' Trevor took the remote from next to the candy dish and scrolled through the menu. Nothing interested him. Then he saw a listing for *Drop Outs*, a show about sky-diving instructors. His dad was not on the show, but he did jump people out of planes and pull their parachutes open for a living. Trevor had not seen his dad since the sixth grade but liked to torture himself by watching these guys discuss the risks then laugh all the way down. He selected it.

'I don't want to see that,' his mother said. Trevor changed the channel and went to take a shower.

Celeste's paintings arrived in a cardboard box that took up half of the living room. In one a man's eyes bled ink. In another, a blue woman hurled broken bottles at tiny pink asses in the cloud above her head. Paint streaked. Paint ran in changing directions. Paint took big dumps of more paint. Trevor thought that if Celeste had kept to the abstract stuff he might have found something to like. He might have seen a storm system on Saturn, Jupiter's famous big red spot, solar flares. Instead, he bristled at each rainbow blast of tortured thoughts and hoped his mother wouldn't hang them on the wall.

'Mom, I was all ... effed up when I painted those,' Celeste would say, twisting a hangnail. 'Why d'you even want them?'

The answer was always the same: 'Because you have a gift ...'

and their mom would go on to tell how she had thrown away her own. She had taken years of ballet classes and, at seventeen, danced the part of Medora in the All City youth production of *Le Corsaire*. She had danced it so well that her teacher came into the dressing room afterwards to say that a good, personal friend from years ago, who now taught dance at NYU, was waiting to congratulate her in the foyer. Trevor's mother had worked extremely hard for everyone's approval, but she did not go to the foyer to meet her teacher's friend. She used the rear door to the parking lot and waited for her parents by their car. A week later, she dropped out of the dance school, feeling for the first time that she must have better things to do, sink in with other people, look as bored as possible, chase boys.

Of course, when their mother came to the end of the story, she inverted everything, saying it had all turned out for the best and she would never change what had happened, her two wonderful children. Trevor knew his mother's ballet story, and it always made him sad. It always worked on him.

Soon their mother took Celeste out for a 'mother–daughter day', and they came home with two oversized bags of new used clothes. Not just jeans and tops and shoes but black dress pants and black collared shirts.

'Your sister found a job,' Trevor's mother said.

'I'm gonna waitress,' Celeste smiled, her chipped tooth miraculously whole. 'At the same place as you.'

Trevor thought of the servers at Gianni's Italian Restaurant, where he washed dishes three evenings a week. They did everything a lot faster than Celeste. Maybe it had been his mother's idea, her way of making him get more involved, probably as an informant.

When Celeste did not show up for her third shift, Gianni asked if Trevor knew why.

'I don't know. I'm really sorry,' he said. He wanted to say, 'You think that's my sister? Yeah, right!' Instead, he agreed to tell her: 'Gianni says don't bother coming back.'

That night, Trevor woke to a twang and sudden brightness. Celeste had poked a needle through his doorknob and sprung the lock. He sat up, pulling the covers high, scared she would see him naked, though he always wore pajamas to bed. She swayed a little, her head to one side, like a zombie, her odour reminding him of the storage room to his school's biology lab, except the floor would have to be one giant ashtray.

'You tell on me?'

'No,' he said, squinting at the safety pin open between her fingers. He had not said anything. He had avoided their mother all evening, lying that he wasn't hungry and needed to work on a school project. 'I didn't,' he said.

Celeste nodded, glancing around his room. The two magazine cut-outs over his desk caught her eye: one a hot pink and purple composite image of a supernova, the other a photograph of a girl in a wetsuit with a longboard held upright beside her. Along the bottom of the advertisement was the name of the surf shop, Crest King's, printed in a wave shape. Justin, the shop-owner, knew that Trevor had been saving all his earnings for a hand-built board.

'I went to school with that girl,' Celeste said. 'She was so fat we used to call her Earthquake, but she's lost most of it. Must be forcing her meals back up.' She jabbed her middle finger towards her mouth and clicked her throat. Trevor remained quiet. Until that moment, the girl in the picture had not looked fat or skinny to him. Now she was both.

Each day, his mother seemed so happy to give Celeste fifteen dollars against her first pay cheque. Trevor couldn't bring himself to tell her there would never be one. He could not even tell her when she asked, revealing undercurrents of doubt, if Celeste was in fact still going to her job. He lied until Celeste blew her own cover a week later. She'd forgotten all about the restaurant. She must have started thinking of the money as her allowance. Trevor couldn't believe how stupid this was. When she stormed out, leaving them alone in the kitchen, his mother reached across the table and pulled his dinner plate away from him. Trevor didn't argue. He snatched a piece of bread and went to his room, slamming the door behind him.

He had seen the board at a surf competition the summer before and stared and stared at it while other spectators stopped, nodded and wandered away. Eventually, the man with salt-and-pepper hair down to his shoulders sitting at the back of the booth took an interest in him. He told Trevor about saving up for his own first-ever board at about the same age. 'And I still use that one all the time, which is saying something, considering how many I've got. By the way,' he said, putting out his hand, 'I'm Justin.'

But when, the Saturday after Celeste quit her pretend job, Trevor and his mother arrived at Crest King's and Justin knew exactly which board to bring out, Trevor could not find his bank card. It was not in his wallet or his pockets. He did not understand. He had used it to check his online account the night before to make sure it was all there, the last installment of forty dollars. Where could it have gone? His mother looked disappointed, but handed Justin a card of her own and said, 'This one should work.' Trevor wished she wouldn't. He wanted to go straight home and search their apartment. His mother reminded him, however, that she seldom drove this way. He would just have to give her the money later, when he had found his card.

To Justin, it would appear that Trevor's mother had been paying for his board the whole time, in installments because she could hardly afford it. He would class Trevor as the type of kid who always got his way.

'Celeste took it,' Trevor said, once they were back in the car.

'What are you talking about?'

'My card, she stole it.'

'Don't jump to conclusions,' his mother said. 'You should know better.'

'No, *you* should. Celeste is fucked.'

'What did you just say?'

'I said, Celeste is a *fucking loser*.' He waited for his mother to hit the brakes and scream him out of the car. But she only looked ahead at the road and followed it home.

Once there, she locked herself into the bathroom. Trevor could hear her crying from his room, where he found the missing bank card under his bed. He thought of his sister flicking the beer cap at him. He could not stay there any more. He biked to his friend Tim's house.

Early the next morning, Tim's dad took the boys fishing on the ocean with a lot of other men. Trevor caught a fifteen-inch flounder, and when the fish flapped out of the water, a good catch, all the men cheered. Someone passed him a can of beer. Someone else slapped him heartily on the back.

When school let out on Monday, Trevor biked to the gift shop where his mother worked. He had texted her on Saturday evening to say where he would be then switched off his phone. They had not spoken all weekend, nor had he wanted to. After Celeste moved in, his mother had been treating him differently, like someone who must fit a certain mould or go unloved. If his few needs now irked her, if he had become such a burden, couldn't he move out west to live with Dad? Couldn't he be the one to decide whose expectations made any sense?

She was flattening boxes in the back room of the shop when he arrived. He watched her for a minute, waiting for her to stop working so he wouldn't have to shout. He didn't want to cry. Then she looked up, and he realised by her surprise that she hadn't heard him come in, and now she did all the talking.

'I'm sorry, Trev. Your sister's made so many bad choices. It's like she's determined to ruin her own life. But I've still got you, right? I know your head's on straight. So at least I've still got one good kid.' Her eyes filled with tears, and Trevor felt himself drift towards her, wrap his arms around her soft waist. He began to mumble, 'Everything's okay, Mom. Everything's fine,' a wide surface opening inside him, a type of numbness that unfurled and held his whole world at a distance, like a canopy of good, strong cloth. When his mother had stopped shaking, he went to find a box of tissues while she closed up the shop.

'Anyway, I've had it with Gretchen,' she said, somewhat cheered. Gretchen was her boss. 'She won't let me put any of your sister's paintings on display. Says they're too disturbing. On the way home, maybe we can stop by some other places, see if they'll hang one or two? It would be so good for Celeste's self-esteem.'

Trevor put the tissues down beside his mother's purse and stared at the stack of paintings leaned behind the counter. On the outermost, a pair of dentures clenched a blue apple. Around the apple and from within, a set of smoke-grey rings gaped moons of terrified eyes. As his mother finished counting the cash in the register, he picked up the canvases and carried them out to the car.

YEHUDIT

PAULA MCGRATH

udy shifts and swallows her way out of sleep, brushes at the damp patch where she drooled on her cheek with the back of her hand. Her ankles come into focus where she has them raised on a footstool. Swollen. Around her, the dogs are yelping, wanting out. One of them might have done something already in the house, there's that smell again. Frank will go nuts. He hates the dogs, and he'd as soon lift one of them with his foot when he's passing as not. She'd better straighten the place out, not go giving him reasons.

Besides, it's Tuesday.

She hauls herself out of the chair, scattering the coupons and newspapers she forgot were in her lap. Frank hates her coupons. Says he doesn't need food stamps, thank you very much. She gave up explaining the difference long since. Besides, he already knows the difference; he's just being contrary. She keeps cutting the coupons because she can save five or ten dollars a shop, but since Frank drives her to the store, she never gets to use them. She must have ten cookie tins full by now, most all of them out of date. She plans to sort them out one of these days.

She puts the dogs out, but she's wheezing hard from the exertion. It's the weight that slows her down. She didn't always used to be this heavy. She really should try and reduce – Now where did she put that darn … She finds her inhaler, in the pocket of her muumuu where it should be, takes three short puffs. This darn heat. Tugging the synthetic fabric free where her dress has stuck to her thighs, she shuffles to turn the AC up a notch. That ought to do it. Should be nice and cool in time for the kids' lessons. The kids. A whoosh of well-being washes over her, and the heat isn't bothering her nearly as much.

Tuesdays are good. After Paulie Walsh – bless the child, music is for everyone, and he has just so much energy, but he is completely without talent – after Paulie's lesson, it's Kane. And after Kane … As usual, Judy has no one coming after Kane. She likes to let his time run on as long as possible, whenever his mother will allow it. Every lesson culminates in a tiny struggle, because both of them want Kane to keep playing, but Judy knows the mother can't afford more time but is too proud to let his time run without paying. So much potential. And only six. She will have to give him up soon, pass him on to the Music Institute. She worries that the mother won't be able to afford their enormous fees. She will tell her today that they must work hard, stay late, to make sure he wins one of the scholarship places. She's feeling pleased with this plan, but it saddens her too.

There's that prickle behind her eyes again, but she can hardly help it. Kane is so much like her Joseph at the same age. Such talent. It was her mother all over again, playing through his fingers. His gift, his wonderful, wonderful gift. At least he never followed his father into the used-car business, at least she can be thankful for that.

Judy moves around slowly, straightening things out. Tuesdays are good. Joseph is in the city Tuesdays. She knows, because she saw him drive by the house. She was standing by the window, just looking out at nothing, when she saw his van go straight by, without even slowing down. She could not believe it.

– I could not believe it, she exclaimed to Frank that evening. Straight by, without even slowing down. Without even looking at the house. His own home.

– What's not to believe, Frank said from behind the sports page.

– That he could—

– I know what you mean, Frank said levelly. I just don't know why you are surprised, is all.

– Well … Judy was flustered. Frank was right. Joseph never called by. Not unless he really had to. Thanksgiving, Christmas. That was about it.

– Well, I'm going to pick up the phone right now and find

out why a son would not call in to his own mother when he's passing by.

But Frank had raised his paper with that slow deliberateness of his and was no longer listening. No reasonable conclusions could be reached by discussing their son, she ought to know that by now. They each lived with their own private version of disappointment where Joseph was concerned, and there was no overlap. There was nothing left to say on the subject.

She moved to the counter and picked up the phone.

– Um … Joseph said.

–You know, busy … Joseph said.

– Next time … Joseph said.

Judy picked him up on it in a flash.

– Next time you're—

–You know, next time – the wholesaler's …

– So you go to the wholesaler's, every Tuesday.

She could imagine Frank's bushy eyebrows lifting behind his newspaper. And Joseph had conceded that, yes, every Tuesday. Then he modified it to most Tuesdays. Most Tuesdays he was in Chicago at the wholesaler's, and yes, he would, one of the days when he wasn't so busy, stop by to see his mother.

– There, Judy put the phone down with a flourish.

– He's not gonna come over, Frank said, without looking up.

But you never knew, he just might. She doesn't know when she saw him last. He's just so darn busy. Frank drives out there sometimes. He doesn't go to see his son. He goes to keep an eye on his investment. Well, maybe next time she will surprise them both, take a drive out with him. Soon as the weather cools down a bit. The fall, maybe. It's nice, being in the nature when the leaves are turning. Yes, that's what she's going to do.

She lowers her bulk onto the piano stool, smiling as she imagines herself in the passenger seat of Frank's Cadillac, leaving Chicago behind, heading out on the open road into the heart of mid-western America. She will take that tour of Joseph's farm, try out some of his vegetables. She wonders what might be in season in the fall. Corn? Pumpkin? She will make Mother's pumpkin challah. She can already see herself, taking the hot yeasty loaves out of Joseph's oven. But then she remembers. No challah. Mother is long gone, but Frank is of the same mind as her mother. No Jewish cooking. No Jewish anything. Funny how she can't seem to get it into her head, even after all these years.

She glances at the clock. If Joseph is coming, he'd better hurry, because the children will be here soon. He'd never come after, not if there's any chance Frank might be there. Poor Joseph, having to take a loan from Frank that time. It must have killed him. No, they do not get on. She does not want to think about them, toe to toe, not getting on.

Maybe she will make him pumpkin pie instead when she takes that drive out. They'll sit in Joseph's kitchen, filled with cinnamon smells, and talk. In her mind's ear they are talking in

German. But that would never happen, not with Frank around. She wonders if Joseph remembers, when he was little, chatting away to her in the language she was not able to forget, even when Mother insisted. That was when he was still playing piano. When he still chatted to her. The happiest time of her life.

Her fingers have crept onto the keyboard, remembering a jolly little song, one of the very first Joseph learned. He played it by ear when he was hardly more than three. Straight in, starting at an F. But then she plays A-flat, not the A that belongs to the tune. With B, C, dissonant, melancholic, unfinished.

Yehudit is six. They have been walking for a long time. She is tired, but Mother is even more tired so she carries her own small bag. In it is a piece of hard bread, and the photograph. Then there is a train, then more walking. It seems to be night for a long time, and it is still dark when they reach the end of the road. A wooden bridge is slung across black water to a boat. Mother flinches when the man there puts out his hand to help her across. He pulls his hand back, says something in a language Yehudit does not understand, steps a little away. Mother seems very tall and all alone as she walks across. She does not hold the ropes, even though the bridge rocks and sways.

The boat takes a long time. She plays with the other children, Adam, Solomon. She can't remember the other girl's name. They hide all over, even in the Captain's quarters. He is nice to them and smiles a lot, but still he seems sad.

She is American now, Mother tells her, with one of those same, sad smiles. This will be their home, this small apartment with one bedroom, a toilet on the landing. She does not know why Mother cries the day the knock comes on the door and the two American men bring in a piano.

– There ya go, missy, one of them says, mussing Yehudit's hair.

But the piano is not for her, it is for Mother, and she cries when she plays it, probably because she is remembering the pretty dress, the tall handsome man leaning on another, big, shiny piano, smiling down at her while she played: the people in the photograph.

Mother was sad the day Yehudit came home from school crying because everyone was speaking in English and she did not understand what they were saying.

– You will, Yehudit. In time you will understand.

She said it like You-dith. Except at school they said Ju-dith. The teacher even spelled it wrong in the roll book.

She made some friends after a while. Wait up, Jude, they called, rushing to link arms on the way to school, the way girls do. Only, Mother heard Wait up, Jew. Judith tried to explain, but it didn't matter. From then on, Mother stopped observing the holiday and reading the Torah, and Yehudit became Judy. Mother looked sad again when she heard Judy's friends call her. It was impossible to make Mother happy.

Later, when Judy got in from school, Mother was tired as well as sad. She had to cut back her hours at the store where she worked, but before long she was too tired even for that. When she was too ill to work any more, Judy said goodbye to high school and her friends and stayed home to look after her. Even when she had done everything, helped her to take sips, to swallow her pills, cleaned her up, fixed her pillows, she could tell that Mother was still in pain. She didn't say anything, but Judy could see it in her eyes. Then, when she could not take the pain away with pills or comfortable pillows, Judy played piano. Mother had been a patient teacher, and Judy a good, though not gifted, pupil, and as she stroked the keys into melodies from her mother's past, a temporary peace crept into the apartment, enveloping them both.

When there was no more money, sixteen-year-old Judy did not know where to turn. The neighbour across the hall was good to them, but she had not much herself. Go to Maxwell Street, she told Judy. There, old man Rosenberg would give her cash for anything she had to sell. Judy went. She put her head down and wove her way through the pandemonium of up-turned boxes and crates heaving with their wares, the cacophony of accents, German, Irish, Italian, and plenty more she did not recognise, peddling lamps, television sets, bikes, strange-smelling clothes, all competing with the sliding blue notes of harmonicas and guitars. The pullers called to her, tugged on her sleeve, tried to entice her in to the stores. She drew her coat more tightly around her and hurried on until she found it: Rosenberg's Jewellery.

He was about a hundred, but he was the one sitting her down and getting her water to drink.

– There, he said in Hebrew. You feel better, eh?

Judy nodded, still feeling weak, not trusting herself to speak, in any language.

– You are Laila's girl? he asked gently.

Judy nodded again.

– She is not well, I hear.

She shook her head.

– Laila, Laila, it took all her strength from her.

Judy did not know what he meant, but the old man was talking more to himself than to her.

– Terrible, terrible, he was saying. Terrible times. All the poor little children. Poor Laila. Poor Jacob.

Then he seemed to remember again that she was there.

– I knew your grandfather, he said softly, and he counted out far too many dollars in exchange for her mother's watch.

When there was nothing else, Judy sold the piano, and when her mother begged with her eyes for some music, Judy could only stare at her hands where they sat palm up in her lap, her fingers as useless as the flailing legs of an upturned beetle.

When her mother died, Mr Grube, the store-owner, took

pity on her and gave Mother's old job to Judy, though she knew nothing at all about counting and measuring, and she was too quiet to be any good with the customers. But she turned up in good time every day with her face well scrubbed and hair in a tidy braid, ready and willing to do her best. When a certain Frank Martello started coming often, the owner winked and told her she'd want to look out for those Italians. After that, Judy blushed every time he came in. She fumbled his change and stammered answers to his questions, so it came as a complete surprise when he leaned his elbow on the counter and asked her how she'd like to come work for him, in a nice office job. Mr Grube joined in from the storeroom.

– You going to pay her well, eh?

– I'll double her wages, Frank replied, quick as a shot, with a wink to Judy, who blushed to the soles of her feet.

– Then get outta here fast as your feet can carry you, Judy, Mr Grube said.

Frank was as good as his word. He gave her such an easy job that she wondered if he thought she was an idiot, but she was happy to hide away in the quiet office behind his own at the back of the lot. Every day he came in for a chat, to put her at her ease. He was such a talker. That was why he was so good at selling cars. He talked her into filling in at reception before long, and when she protested that she couldn't possibly, looking down at her faded skirt and well-washed sweater, he took her by the two hands and danced her out of the office and into one of the fancy sporty cars, the best in the showroom.

– Then we're going down town, pretty lady.

He brought her to State Street, to the famous Marshall Field's.

– Pick out whatever you want, Frank said grandly.

Judy had never set foot inside the door of Marshall Field's before. The doorman intimidated her, the perfumes overwhelmed her, and she hardly dared to lift her eyes.

When Frank noticed, he grabbed a saleswoman by the arm.

– My girl here could use a little help finding something nice.

That was the first day he called her his girl. Frank could be kind back then. He bought her a caramel twinset and a mustard dirndl skirt and a box of Frango mints.

After they got married, Frank didn't like her working in the lot any more.

– What do you want, hanging around those guys all day? he asked, and she didn't have an answer to that. She didn't have answers to many of the questions husbands ask because she had never heard them answered; she did not remember her father and mother together, only in the photograph. She spent her days in their new home on the South Side. She was lonesome, but she told herself they would soon fill those empty bedrooms.

The bedrooms stayed empty, and Judy found it harder to count her blessings every day. Living with Mother had been like living with a shadow, moving silently about, getting everything done with the least amount of fuss. Frank was the opposite. He never talked when he could shout, he left doors open, and the television was on from the time he got up in the morning and again from the moment he got home, with the volume up high. It took some getting used to.

Sometimes she didn't know she was crying, and when he'd ask her what in tarnation was the matter she'd have to put a hand to her cheek and feel it wet to realise. When he looked into her dark eyes she could see his incomprehension, but she also knew that he did not want to understand what he saw in there; he did not want to know what her dark eyes had seen. He covered his fear with impatience, then with anger, so the house swung between oppressive silences and frustrated outbursts, frequently followed by a slamming door, then silence again.

– What? Frank asked her when he came back from whatever bar he'd gone to. What do you want from me?

He sat heavily onto their bed, where she lay with her back to him, her face pressed into her damp pillow.

– What do you want, Judy? he asked, more gently.

She whispered it, so he didn't hear at first.

– Ya what?

She lifted her head so he could hear better.

– A piano.

Frank liked people to know he could afford the best. He pulled the blankets off with a flourish.

– What do you think, Judy? Think this'll make her happy, boys? he asked the delivery men, his audience. They were standing back, two Irishmen, letting him have his moment, probably hoping for a tip. What do you say we get her to give us a tune? What about one of Johnny Ace's. Come on, baby. Never Let Me Go. Can't have these boys saying you weren't worth the top of the range.

Judy had never played for anyone except her mother before, and she could feel her hands trembling. She moved to the piano, then looked around her vaguely.

– A stool …?

Frank's look turned dark, until he spotted the smaller object by the door. Then he was all smiles again.

– A stool, boys. Give the lady a stool.

The stool was unveiled and placed behind her.

Judy knew the melody; Frank was fond of playing it in his car at full volume. She brought her fingers to the smooth ivory, releasing a single pure note with only the lightest of touches, and another. Then another, all in minor thirds. There was something in the resonance that fixed them all in the stillness, made even Frank shut up. Then, when the last whisper of the chord died away, Judy's right hand picked out the melody they wanted to hear, and her left hand joined in with the simple runs the song required. Forget about tomorrow, my darling … never let me go, Frank accompanied her loudly, off-key.

On their way down the front steps, after pocketing a five-dol-lar bill, one of the movers said under his breath, feckin' eejit, and something about shooting himself. Judy didn't find out until later that they were talking about the singer, Johnny Ace, who had shot himself with an accidentally loaded gun.

The house became filled with the music Mother had taught her. Frank complained that it always sounded sad, but she couldn't help it, the melancholy seemed to go further back than she did, maybe back to her mother, growing up in a place Judy didn't know, and couldn't imagine. Or couldn't remember. But it was what she heard resonating in her ear. She had to remember to wipe the tears away before Frank came home. Though she wasn't unhappy, he would not understand.

Then Joseph came. Judy played him into being. He was dark-eyed and dark-skinned, and Frank said he was the image of the Napoli Paolinis on his mother's side, but Judy knew he was of her. As soon as he could reach the keys, he played. At two or three he copied what she showed him, her shadow treble, her shadow bass.

By the time he was six, Joseph could play Mahler as well as his small hands would allow. Though he didn't understand the music, the feeling of angst, seeping from the fingers of his small son, made Frank frown. Judy taught Joseph to play Debussy's *Feuilles Mortes* and Ravel's dreamy, melancholic *Oiseaux Tristes* instead. Frank still grumbled, not understanding, but he left them alone.

The day before Joseph's seventh birthday, they were doing finger exercises, Joseph speeding up and down the keyboard in finger-perfect semitones. Every note was a dart in Judy's flesh, because she was preparing Joseph for the Music Institute entrance exams; he was too good for her. They had already come out to hear him play, the President of the Institute himself and a woman. They had stopped in the porch – Judy saw them through the window – listening to Joseph practising. They shook their heads, and looked at each other, and nodded their heads. This was all before they even pressed the bell. The exam was a formality, they said, when they were leaving.

Up and down the keyboard, four octaves, Joseph's tongue protruded slightly in concentration. Neither of them saw it coming: the little hands, side-swiped off the keys, the lid slammed down. Frank looked at them while the wood resounded in their ears, daring them. In his hand he held a mitt and a ball and a bat.

– That stuff's for little kids, Joey. Little kids and sissies. It's Little League from now on. Time to forget about all that music.

Judy has a surprise planned. Young Kane will make a start on the Symphony No. 5 piano transcription, Mahler. Half-German, that's what his mother said when they first came. It was close enough. The mother was Japanese, and she had sought Judy out, having heard of her reputation from Kane's school. Kane stood beside her, serious and quiet, while Judy explained to his mother, who wanted him to learn the Suzuki method, that she could only teach the method she learned from her mother. It didn't have a name, she said.

Her fingers are giddy with anticipation, but before she can tease the keys with the opening bars, the doorbell rings. Paulie Walsh. As she goes to let the child in she sets aside the familiar, dull disappointment that precedes the child's lesson every Tuesday – because another week has passed that Joseph didn't come – and she fills the vacant place with enough justifications to make it right.

Paulie is red-haired and freckled, and he looks, as always, with his hair sticking out and his clothing all askew, as if he just fell from a tree house. He makes Judy think of that show Joseph used to like to watch, *Leave It to Beaver*.

– How are you, Paulie? Judy asks, with a wave to Paulie's mother, who is waiting in the car.

– Ya know, Mrs M., same ol', same ol'.

Judy laughs.

– I hope not, she says. You promised you would practise this week.

– Yes, Mrs Martello, Paulie says, his step losing some of its bounce.

Judy lets him have a go at his piece, a simple little tune he's been torturing for months now, and, as expected, it doesn't go well.

– Let's try this, she says. We'll sing it. I'll sing first – lala lala laaa – now you …

– La la la la la, Paulie intones miserably.

– Lala lala laaa? Judy tries again.

– La la la la la.

Judy inhales, then slowly exhales. She was getting too old for this. If it wasn't for Kane—

– Clapping, she says. We'll try clapping out the music, Paulie. It's all about rhythm. Let's go.

But the clapping is a failure too. Judy glances at the clock. Too soon to let him out to his mother. She will have to have a chat with her one of these days.

The piece is illustrated with lambs, frolicking on a hillside.

– I know, Judy says. Colour. We will colour the picture.

She lumbers to the sideboard to rummage for materials. Paulie gives her a cynical look, which changes to resignation when he, too, glances at the clock. To its too-slow, metronomic increments Paulie scratches away at the lambs with a crayon.

– Thanks, Mrs M., Paulie calls, as he bounds down the steps.

– Practise, Paulie, Judy says, as she waves him off.

She is already distracted, looking up and down the road to see if there is any sign of Kane. His mother usually walks with him from Grand Station. Usually, they are there, waiting on the steps. They are never late.

She goes back inside eventually, not wanting the neighbours

to witness her anxious waiting. She's wheezing again. Her inhaler – Where is it? Ah. She takes three puffs. She waits. She looks at the photograph on the piano, her beautiful mother looking at her father looking back at her as she plays. The only sounds in the front room come from the second hand of the clock, pressing relentlessly forward into the second half of Kane's lesson, and the faraway whine of her own inhalations.

PAPRIKA

FRANK McGuinness

I f you were to put a gun to my head and demand I tell you what I believe to be the loveliest aria in all opera, I think I would surprise you. You could not guess my answer in a million years. I can hear obvious choices being recited. Perhaps you would be able to show off and tell me it is some hidden piece buried in an obscure work you chanced upon hearing in some little village festival you stumbled across in the wilds of Ireland or in the reclaimed wetlands of some Dutch province. Maybe I too came upon this wonderful gem and am sent here to agree with you, to confirm your choice, to prove that as in my own art there is fate, a force of destiny intent on bringing us together, we who share such an esoteric taste in beauty.

You would be wrong to assume so. I take no pleasure in closing that gate to you. I do not allow you to enter, invited through to my room – make yourself comfortable, kick your shoes off, you know what we like to listen to in it. But you cannot be my welcome guest for you don't have permission to come into my house, my company. I do not give you the key. I do not know who you might find prowling there, walking the feet off himself, tiring the day and night out of his limbs so that sleep might at least – a little sleep might even be possible. Who knows what exhausted breathing might follow your footsteps? Who might be on the very brink of expiring in your arms should you dare to cross my threshold? Better to be refused entry – to be denied any access. So, as I say, I do not give it to you and already I owe you an apology for misleading you.

This is how I madden my friends. I make a statement that I am about to reveal something about myself – then I stand back at the last minute and say nothing. It is an appalling habit. Perhaps it accounts for my coldness. For why I rarely married. Women's flesh now bores me, and men's has always disgusted me. I live apart. I am honest enough to admit that I prefer the sound of my own voice. Am I alone in making clear that preference? When it comes to my voice, am I flattering myself when I say it is in demand? I shall not bore with the names of leading companies where I have performed and continue to perform. There is a type of singer whose list of roles is their sole topic of conversation. You can hear their soprano sweetness even as I accuse. A little of that company is sufficient. Whatever else may be made of my arrogance, I can argue I learned my lesson well from these ladies. I avoid talk about opera when I can.

I admit this is because I find so few people capable of interesting me on the subject – they simply lack the verbal accuracy to speak with any degree of intelligence about music. It descends almost always into what I truly despise: gossip, which is all most criticism comes down to, if truth be told. The squalid daydreams of some silly queen longing to try on some diva's frock, masquerading as the lush lyricism of a Puccini expert, dying to expire as Butterfly, pining onto death for his Pinkerton. Then there are the academics. The odour of pipes, the grey of their beards, the rot of their teeth and breath, the unreadable analysis, the technical mysticism, all of it hiding the deepest ignorance, all of it disguising the simple truth – they do not understand their subject. Inevitably, by their side, the not quite pretty girl or boy, accompanying the ageing master, ever ready for the ride, the kamikaze screw that will disfigure them for life, disfigure them sufficiently to take up the teaching profession.

That is why I make a point of never thanking my teachers. I have been known to race from funeral services rather than to shake the hand of any one of them. I once risked nearly jumping into the open grave to avoid these creatures. I would certainly never go to any of their farewells. I did hear of a Jamaican professor whose relatives insisted his mourners, family and friends, his former pupils, actually dig the earth he was to lie in – I do not fancy dirtying my soft hands in that way. Certainly not for anyone who wasted my time and energy. They all know this. I have never received even a word of congratulations from that jealous shower. It is not that I need nor have looked for such encouragement. I presume my quote, made in an interview, deeply offended. I dared to say I succeeded despite them. Yes, I know it is the kind of predictable joke a clever schoolboy might crack. I was never acknowledged to be clever as a boy. I was never considered special in any way. My instrument was judged to be merely promising, and not especially so. There were fellows in my class who were expected to surpass me. They are now teaching beginners. So, if it were a juvenile insult, I am the happier for that. Really, do they need to take it so seriously? I heard – believe me, I so frequently heard – that I had hurt them. Well, it was my intention to do so. They might have believed that as I aged I would mellow and recover the modesty they had so abused in my childhood and teenage years, suffering under their complacency, learning what took me too many years to discard as utterly worthless in my pursuit of my full voice, my full soul and self. They could whistle for all I cared. Not my way, I'm afraid. Not my style.

And what is that? I like perfection. And, to me, the perfect piece of music, the one I would most like to sing – it is in the very opera I came to deliver in the Big Apple. This is not my first Otello. I shall not reveal to you how many times I have sung it. It is obvious there are only so many performances one voice can despatch in that role. Suffice to say, I am not within spitting distance of that total. There is life in the old tar yet. It is imperative to let your Iago and Desdemona know this. You do so by allowing them to believe that for all your fame, your reputation, your stature, your size – you are a jolly fellow, you are a good sport. I tell them, truthfully, my favourite aria is the Willow Song, Desdemona's pathetic cry before she is strangled, as she remembers a maid called Barbara, a girl martyred by a lover who has now deserted her and left her to go mad. I am naturally not alone in adoring Verdi's genius as it caresses and disturbs me through that shattering lament. But there must be, I am sure, few celebrated tenors who for the amusement of their fellow troupers can sing it. It is quite extraordinary that now, in my hefty fifties, I can resort to a near parody of my boyhood's beautiful voice – even the threatening break – the disfiguring – I can make an uncanny fist of it.

> *Piangea cantando nell'erma landa,*
> *Piangea la meste.*
> *O Salce! Salce! Salce!*

Bravo, Iago praises. Brava, the conductor smiles to correct him. Desdemona throws back her golden hair and sings, 'O willow, willow, willow!' Does the silly bitch think I cannot translate *salce*? Then I speak, asking, as Desdemona does, who is knocking at the door? In ridiculous falsetto, Iago answers as Emilia does, 'E il vento', it is the wind. I resume my boyish brilliance.

Io per amarlo e per morire.
Cantiamo! Cantiamo!
Salce! Salce! Salce!

I eye Desdemona. I wait for her to translate. 'I love him and I will die. Let us sing, let us sing, willow! willow! willow!' I wait in vain. She is strangely quiet. She joins in the generous applause, but she alone knows I am not joking. She will perform this exquisite hymn to female weakness. The house will listen to a woman abandoned, perfectly pathetic. Then I will arrive onstage, her ravager, her rope around the neck, the beautiful twist and chain of neck, the weeping face, the eyes darkening beneath the pillow. She will not fear that I might actually kill her. No, she will see in my own eyes, hear in my voice that I mock her. I have more regard for my mockery of the role than her sweet relish of its music. I would make a better Desdemona than she could ever sing, bound and big as I am, perfectly cast as Otello. It is my mission to destroy this woman, throttle her, leave her voice shattered, changed beyond recognition for the rest of her career. Desdemona is born to die, and I know how to do it, how to be her killer, sing her to death. That is my job. She knows it as well. That is why, when I finished my mimicking party piece, all through rehearsal, she never takes her eyes off me. So attentive is she to me, I am sure word must be spreading through the scandal-addicted orchestra and chorus, there is surely about our attentions all the signs that an affair is beginning.

There isn't. Our soprano was considered to be a beautiful woman, but I had tired of beauty. I had even begun to dislike it. This was when I was friends with a photographer – in those days I was not choosy. He could wield a camera like a butcher's knife, cutting girls into glamorous glory, and yet the man was effectively a eunuch. He hated the female of the species. I was most fascinated in his many affairs when they were ending. He would begin to remind these women incessantly that they were ageing. He was deeply in love with the speed of his vision. He would tell me in wonderful confidence when each love was on the point of collapse. He would start to profess to her that he had always confused love with sorrow. The women would begin to receive a rose that had started to wither. It would be delivered at exactly the right instant of her discontent with him. Then he would vanish from her life. Vanish completely, even though he'd tied the knot with a few.

All right, I was that man. In those days I did dabble with a camera. But I had no ambitions there. I shared the secrets of my love life to a sympathetic couple in their restaurant – Hungarian – where I would eat alone, scorning any company but that man and his wife. She was first to notice I'd put on a little weight. But my voice was improving as my girth was gaining. For a man who loathed cliché, this one of the fat tenor I actually enjoyed.

Still, she advised me not to grow too heavy. She passed on to me an old Danube secret. Sprinkle paprika, as much paprika as you can tolerate, on everything you eat. That controls your diet. You will eat less. Again, it had the opposite effect on me. I had found my addiction, my potion, my elixir. I could not get enough of it. Smear a chicken with paprika. Inside and outside. The flesh cooks like the sun. I'd devour it. The spice seemed to break into my bones, my blood, my brain, into my singing, so that it burned with warmth, it loved the sound of itself, it healed the sick and the lame, it fed the multitude of five thousand after five thousand, and had plenty left to feed five thousand more. I had never tasted such a dish. Had never enjoyed such success. Place a plate of an entire bird, a feast of chicken paprika – its breasts, its legs, its wings – I will eat it in one sitting, and for my supper I will find notes of such fulfilment, music of such thanks, a voice you will drink like the reddest, purest wine, quench your thirst with the sweetest, most fragrant white. And I can do this with the lovely, natural means of paprika – doses of paprika – my spice, my drug, my magic. I could not do without it. The food, the weight suited me. Yes, I grew, so did my art. Music more and more marvellous. Offers more and more frequent. Roles increasing in demand. Paprika – it did me no harm whatsoever. I sang my soul – I do believe a singer must bare his soul. Blacks are right to call their music soul. Although they weren't black, the boy and girl, lying on Fifth Avenue, making strange moan.

That is where I saw them, he lying against a yellow wall of an apartment building. She had her head on his stained lap. I was walking from the Waldorf – I know it has gone down, but I still love the old girl, gliding through that golden foyer, the bar's strong, stinging martinis, the bad manners of the rude staff – none of that has changed, and, strangely enough, in New York, that city of constant crises, I like stability. That's why I enjoy walking everywhere. And I adore its opera house. On my first engagement, the doorman confused me, asking if I were here with the construction company doing extensive renovations on the building. That was a joke grown soon stale, sorry was I to have cracked it only once, but never let forget it. Now in the bowels of the Met, grown so familiar I might as well have built its nooks and crannies, I love to trawl through the labyrinths of corridors, so marvellously easy to get lost in, its highways and byways, able to stroll for miles through the ghost city buried beneath the Lincoln Centre, giving what might be my best performances as I serenade the dust and the dead I sense are hiding in that haunted building. As I ramble there, I imagine I sing to my dying father, that enormous man grown thin, eaten by Alzheimer's, endlessly trekking through the prison of his hospital, remembering what he alone could remember, starving to death, demanding he'd dine on nothing but long forgotten food and drink, wishing to give up his ghost, for life was now nothing. I hope he could listen to me pour my heart and soul out, knowing he is dead and hears nothing. He is only cinders and ash.

When I myself die I would like my ashes to be thrown into the Met's great fountain. I would like its towering waters to be the only tears shed for me. I have found that mourning is a desperate waste of time. My parents would both have agreed with me on that. We're born, we breathe, we die, we're dirt. It is utter nonsense to feel the need to grieve. We should all be cut from tougher rock. Wailing is ridiculous. It is what theatre – what opera – was invented for, so we can dispense with such conduct. The stage is the best place for such behaviour. Weeping is written out for you. You perform, and the task of tears is done. Sorrow is finite here. It is efficient. It is clean. You make your song and dance, and that's it over. That is why it would be so convenient if I were to pass away on stage in New York at the grand Metropolitan Opera. Of course that shall not happen. Life is never that lucky. And I have had my great share – my more than fair quota – of luck – my paprika – it has granted me, that sacred powder, all I can wish. Do not ask for more.

What were they asking for, the boy and girl in the street? What was the crying boy asking? What was his girl listening to, as she sleeps by him, her dreams the stuff of the boy's delirium? Could he be on something? I know nothing about drugs. I detest any lack of control. If I am to admit any addictive weakness, let it be solely paprika. Natural, nourishing, gentle as milk. I would feed it to these hungry children, but they would spit its goodness back at me and even might turn this goodness into something wickedly infected with the saliva of the damned. Is that what they are? Is it some demon who moves through them? I could not tell for sure. The boy's voice was one long litany, a list of gibberish, unrelenting, pouring from his shaking head, her a bag of silent bones, still, always still, asleep on his knees. To my shock I started to believe that his voice was singing in Russian – could it be Russian? No, I could now decipher it was English. He was definitely speaking in English. For some reason I reckoned I should be afraid of his nonsense.

Die boy die stupid fuck
You father what will you do
No child screaming
Ridiculous
Family listen
Hard luck story
Fortune telling
Do this favour
Bred into you
Be hard honest we are honest
He touched my throat
My cock
My father forgive

Bearing grudge

The bastard denied me

Me chapter and verse

Help me

Help me

Help me

Help me please

Do you know what the smell is

Smelly bastard

Shitty pissy smelly bastard

Sniffing powder

Orange powder

Being asked if children sure I do

It turns me

Your child turns

Why not ring

Friends

They answer things

Sniffing

Fuck off

Who is she on my lap

Red hair all short

She is who I am

Passing sentence

We recognise you

Singing lessons

Dutiful son

Help me

Help me

Die boy die stupid fuck

You father what will you do

No child screaming

Ridiculous

Family listen

Hard luck story

Fortune telling

I am walking to the New York branch of Fauchon, my first port of call in Paris, that shop where food is the rainbow, the pot of gold, myrrh and frankincense, all bright with tastes. Hell, I'd pay fifty bucks for a pint of its milk. So much do I adore its delicacies, I'd smear myself with its mustards, perfume myself with its oils – fuck it, since I gave up sex, the place is my porn site, there is where I get my hard-on, so I thread through its pleasure dens slowly, daily, all those classy French people, sitting in Manhattan, sipping coffee. Could I place something brown in the bottom of those fancy little cups, and make them drink paprika, then they would stand up and fill the air with good cheer, blasting into the neighbourhood the news that I am like them, well-fed, content, searching for – searching – looking

for – what? I know what I look after. What I must look after. I
am a sensible man, who must look after his throat. His precious
jewel. His bread and honey. I must stock up on honey – superb
for the voice. The jams, the matchless sweet nougats. Now that
I more or less disdain drink, they are my reward after the opera.
The reason I adore nougat is that I associate it with my childhood. It was cheap as tuppence then. I loved its white chew
with the pink stripe through the white. As a child, I could put it
between my teeth and pull – such pleasure. My teeth then were
white and my tongue pink. I had to use my tongue and teeth
to sing. The boy and girl I noticed on Fifth Avenue, were they
turning into something pink and white? Turning into me? Into
my father? My father, he used enter me in talent competitions.
The boy and girl, to the best of my knowledge, they do not
beg. If I did well in these competitions, my father would stay
sober – that was how he rewarded me. I've convinced myself
this young couple is harmless. My father knew how to make his
son feel wanted. The cops do not move them on, despite their
frequent noise. But if I failed – if the winner were to be decided
by the audience – if the volume of their applause did not merit
me the winner – some pretty tootsie won their fickle heart –
then I would feel the tightening of my throat as I heard them
decisively limit their appreciation of me, by far the best voice
on that stage – and my father would side with them, angry at
my desperation. I want to cross the wide avenue to avoid that

pair. My father put it down to my lack of preparation, that's why I lost, and he'd see to it I would not eat tonight. I do vow, tomorrow, when I take my daily exercise, I will pass them by on the other side until I reach the confectioner. Then I will feast on French sweets.

Their pleasure does not drown his disapproval. He will – I still hear him – voice his – voice – hear his voice. He tells me I am a fat, ugly boy. I take after my mother in my grossness. She too had a sweet voice, so-so, forgettable. When he looks at me, when I fail, I am her son. He tells me, I would disown you if you could not sing. Even your singing will disappoint me. We all know your voice will break. It will vanish. Like your fat, ugly mother, it will be no more. It will die. I start to laugh at him. I hear my mother in my laughter. We will continue laughing at this fool of a father. Sing.

Die boy die stupid fuck

Your father what will you do

No child screaming

Ridiculous

Family listen

Hard luck story

Fortune telling

I stop. Why am I singing this in the middle of Fifth Avenue? Why are people looking? Where are the boy and girl who protect me in this savage town? I have come out without protection. Without paprika. I am at the mercy of my Magyar advisers. What should I do? They say, sing. Go to the opera – sing Otello. That's what you're paid to do. Do it. They talk sense. I do obey. I eat some paprika.

Was I not in such good voice tonight? I question myself because the inevitable compliments from my Desdemona and my Iago are particularly sincere this evening. I know of one ancient lady, now long dead, who had a sure way of unsettling anyone, and letting them know how she would do it. If you were good, the bitch would find some way of upstaging you – a slight cough, a ruffle of a dress, even, if things were going seriously well, a sneeze. If you were bad, she would be still and listen. This night, the pair of them were still as still can be. Perhaps I flatter myself. It was not at me both were looking, nor were they listening to my good self, for in true theatrical fashion, they have surprised everyone. She is an item, with him, and I rejoice for both, particularly her, as I have now had time to study her mournful beauty. Shakespeare described his Desdemona as a white ewe, and myself as a black ram tupping her. With her lengthy face that could be measured in feet if not furlongs, she does have the features of a hungry sheep. Tonight in the Willow Song her voice soared into the tiered echelon of the opera house – the yellow from its gold reflecting like a thousand wedding rings, all threatening to distort me from what I am. Her rendering is greeted with some applause, sympathetic in its way, although I am sure many are willing the strangulation swiftly on its way – a tough shower of bastards at the Met. Ask that of a certain celebrated couple – if you can endure the breath of one. Which, I cannot say, but the Atkins diet does not entirely agree with everyone. All denials have their consequences.

I am scraping Otello's black from my face when temptation struck. What if I did not wash the colour from my body? What if I were to walk out of this dressing room into the silver light of Columbus Circle, my darkness still intact? What if I were to shuffle back to my hotel, a black man in his native city of New York? No, that does not make sense – why would a New Yorker be staying in a hotel when he has a home to go to? What if I were to pretend I was instead a visitor but I come from – where? Make it Washington. I'll hail a cab and ask my bro to show me from the back of his taxi the sights of this magnificent city. I tell him I too drive a cab. This is only the beginning of a serious bond between us, sharing our liking for ladies, knowing what we both mean when we say we like our queers to keep their distance. This leads to tales of failed marriages out of which spring clever children who will someday, God willing, do their daddies proud, and the mamas who reared them – we are big enough to acknowledge that. We also acknowledge our flings with white girls we betrayed because we could not help doing so. We wonder what happens to them, wishing them only luck. We end the night shaking hands, palm against palm. We say we're good guys. The best. By the time I have fully planned this escapade, I am white again. The make-up is removed. I am safe to face the world.

It is a mild night in New York. How rarely that occurs. It is a sure sign something is to happen, something that I cannot control. I give myself to the mercy of events. I cannot stop what comes my way in this perfect weather. Relieved, I will walk the shiny streets of Broadway. Who was ever fool enough to believe they were paved with gold? Well, me for one. And I still do. Beneath the rotten, broken pavements, there are rivers of precious metal, a liquid mine of every mineral, some never yet seen before, and that river of Hades rather than the Hudson is what has truly made New York what it is today, the city where we can be what we want to be. I suppose I should be grateful for the dreams it allows me to possess. Millions of others would be, but I have no thanks, for now all the city does is remind me that dreams are my duty, wishes are my work, and my art is hard slog until my voice breaks again into the crackle of old age and I am forgotten. Then everything starts to fade all about me. I stop recognising where I am. The streets' neon signs turn to blue water and wash them away. The revels, the carnivals of Times Square do not sound in my deafened ears. I may as well be in the Australian desert as here, so parched and cold is the night. I see the great glitter and glamour turn to rack and ruin. The buildings, once so handsome, so virile, have been flattened into dead men. But I know how to walk about this apocalypse. I know where to find food, drink and shelter. It is now very, very late, but in this wilderness many shops open for twenty-four hours. I will soon come across one. I must have been walking miles, but in this town it is always squares and circles, so I have not strayed too far from my hotel. Indeed, at a distance, who can I see?

It is them – there they are – my little twosome. Both on their feet now. Him this time the quiet one, her gorging her thirst from a bottle of whatever is her choice of poison, as they say in London. And she is loud, screaming some snatch of a pop tune, letting the neighbourhood – no, the whole world – know, you'll never get to heaven if you break my heart. Her voice hideous. Her face a mess of freckles. Her red hair dirty as he is dirty, they sway, and he laughs as she screams, look, look who it is – look, I told you I saw him. You didn't believe me. You didn't believe he would come to us, but I saw him, he did come, look. She points me out to the boy, the fat man, the fat man with the beard. Santa Claus. It's him, she runs to me. The boy is now roaring with laughter. Santa – Santa, she calls out. She puts her arms around me. I hurl her aside as if her arms lanced me. I open my throat. I give her my voice at full, terrifying blast. Fuck you don't touch me. Fuck you never touch me. Do not dare touch me.

She is silent for a second. She looks at me as if I've ran-
sacked the breath from her body. As if I've sliced her face in
two. As if I've taken her favourite doll and smashed its plastic
head in. Then her wail breaks. Filth bursts from her lips. You fat
dick. You ugly queer. You piece of pervert shit. I know you – I
know what you are. Cocksucker – cocksucker. I know what you
do. Fat fucking dickhead. I know where you live. I can tell the
cops. I'm going to tell the cops.

She now resumes crying. He joins in, and in duet they label
me, in so far as I can decipher, cocksucker, dick and, many, many
times, motherfucker. But then, in a voice, clear, strong as my
own, the boy warns me again: I'll get the cops, you'll see. You'll
be sorry, I'll get the cops. If my career has taught me anything,
it is to avoid hysteria everywhere but on the stage. It is un-
seemly as … as hunger. It is my mission to quell its pangs, and
I know how to do so. I carry about my person always a small,
plastic portion of my charm, my protector. Paprika. It is what I
pour on that red skull, that freckled face, staining it even more
orange, telling her, be calm, my child. I christen you Paprika
– henceforth your luck shall change, you and your charming
lover. The demon who possesses you, I would free you entirely
of his powers, but that cannot be, for mankind is bound to suffer. We are born to suffer. Let me bless you with the shadow of
my dust. Become my little helper. Protect your sacred self with
most holy spice. Here for you is gold, frankincense, myrrh, call

them paprika, devour it. Anoint all your senses. Cease your lamentation. She yells. The fat fucker's blinded me. What has he put into my eyes? It's burning the sockets out. What has he done to my eyes? I look into her ugly face. She is now pleading to her boyfriend, has he blinded me? If he has, don't let me live. Why did you let him do that to my eyes? If I can't see, end my lousy life. Fucking end it. Just put me down – please, put me down.

I am now well ahead of them. I sneak a look back. She is sobbing in his arms, the sobs mingling with the chant of fat fucker. He reassures her about getting the cops. Their faith in the New York Police Department is not infectious. I feel more than safe enough. I leave them to their revenge. No one could connect me with that pair of tramps. I am a respectable gentleman in an expensive overcoat, his silk blue scarf wrapped wisely around the exquisite instrument of his throat, walking to my suite in the Waldorf hotel, having done a good night's work playing more than a little proficiently one of the most demanding roles in opera. I look for no more credit nor recognition than that. If I had reacted – if I had engaged in any way with those dangerous children I glimpsed – if I had allowed that vermin infest me – who knows what trouble would have followed? And yet I still hear her cry. Put me down – please, put me down. I do believe she moves me to tears. I am sore tempted to sing back.

Io per amarlo e per morire.
Cantiamo! Cantiamo!
Salce! Salce! Salce!

To interrupt would be bad manners. Let the little one have her moment of glory. I am not a vengeful old woman. I keep my silence and stillness even if she is good at this outburst. I will not mock nor push myself centre stage. I will let her weep her heart out. I will console her. I will do as certain tribes in Africa do for women wronged beyond remedy. They are led in scarlet procession to a tree that weeps. Then she may die nobly by her own hand using her red tresses as a rope to break her unfortunate neck. Neither man nor beast shall lay a claw on her corpse. Left to the exposure of the benevolent sun, its light shall turn her flesh to gold. But this gold does not last. And it turns, not to rust, but to paprika. In smearing her thus, in telling this, I forgive her. Perhaps I save her. So I let her weep. Salce, willow, salce. Willow, salce, willow.

THE LETTER

COLIN CORRIGAN

ames was sitting in front of his computer typing his suicide letter when his mother knocked on his bedroom door and, without waiting for an answer, pushed her way in with a tray loaded with lamb cutlets, mashed potato, mushy peas and a pint glass of milk. He stayed facing the monitor, and she left the tray on his bed.

'You sure you don't want to come down and join us?'

'Absolutely.'

She looked up in surprise. 'You will?'

'No. I mean I'm absolutely sure.'

She nodded, but didn't turn to leave. She kept standing there watching him. 'How was work today?'

'Fine, yeah. The same.'

'It's good, that you're keeping busy.'

James smirked. He had spent most of the day sitting in the same seat in the same corner of the Irish Museum of Modern Art, staring into the space between him and a canvas plastered with various shades of teal. He slid the tray onto his lap and began slicing a chop. He felt her still standing there, still watching him. 'What?'

'I was talking to Liz at the range this morning. She says she knows a really good doctor, she gave me his number.'

'A doctor?'

'A therapist.'

'Please don't talk to your friends about me.'

'I worry.'

'Don't.'

She kept standing there. 'Maybe if I made an appointment for you for next Monday?' she said.

'Betty. Your dinner must be getting cold.'

Calling his mother by her given name usually shut her up, and now she turned away and walked down the stairs, leaving the door ajar behind her. He ate as much as he could stomach and went back to work. Seven hours later, just after two in the morning, he typed the last full stop and clicked Print.

'James?'

James opened his eyes and saw Derek's face, beard trimmed neatly around moist lips, paisley cravat puffed up under a sloping chin. He remembered he was at work, and that Derek, his mother's new boyfriend of eleven years, had got him the job.

'I'm awake,' said James.

Derek smiled and spun around with gusto to reveal the painting behind him. *Rose Nocturne* by Philip Taaffe was a tall, rectangular canvas dominated by thin pink lines that seemed to bulge out from the wall like the grooves of an egg slicer.

'It's just an incredible pink, isn't it? And look at those waves,' said Derek. 'So psychedelic.'

'According to the booklet they point to shamanic other-worldism,' said James.

'That's perhaps a little reductive,' said Derek, 'but they're certainly wonderfully transcendental.'

James nodded.

'We've got a directors' meeting now at three o'clock,' said Derek. 'I said I'd pop down and say "Howdy".'

James nodded.

'I'll be driving home at half five, if you want a lift?' said Derek.

'I'll probably have to stay for a while after we close,' said James. 'Sweep the floors and that.'

'That's fine, I can wait for you.' Derek nodded at the art. 'I'm sure I'll find something to amuse me.'

James nodded. Over Derek's shoulder, he saw Shannon breeze her way towards them. She was wearing her purple scarf today. She held her arm an inch above Derek's shoulders and kissed the air next to his face, then turned to James: 'Can you go down to the Response Room?'

'Ah,' said Derek. 'Duty beckons! I'll leave you to it.' He patted Shannon on her elbow and strode off towards the stairs.

'Ethel needs a hand,' she said to James.

'Which one's Ethel?'

'Ethel's the lady who gives the children's workshops.'

'And which one's the Response Room?'

'How long have you been working here?'

James shrugged, and Shannon sighed. 'Downstairs, past reception,' she said.

Shannon had been sighing at his shrugs for almost nine months now. Derek was on the Board and had installed him in his role of general gallery staff member, and James imagined himself a work of performance art, an indictment of nepotism. Shannon and the others, who all knew hosts of unemployed artists who could have done with his job, and who could have done it properly, didn't try to hide their resentment. Or maybe they resented him for other reasons. He didn't blame them.

He walked down the stairs and stopped outside the Response Room. Shrieks and screams leaked out through the half-open door, and James imagined himself turn and flee, through the courtyard and out into the mist that had drifted up from the river. But he had nowhere, real or imagined, to run to.

He opened the door and walked into the commotion. The children were experimenting with modern techniques, creating their own art which seemed to James indistinguishable from the junk on display in the galleries. Ethel, dressed and accessorised like a friendly sorceress, was crouched next to three kids in matching dungarees, and he picked his way through the melee towards her. When she saw him she grabbed his arm and hauled him into the next room.

'Oh thank heaven,' she said. 'We're up to ninety here today. Can you keep an eye on things in here for me? There's more paints and things in the corner, there, and rags to mop up any spills.'

Ethel was somehow able to avoid stepping on a painting or child without watching her feet, and James only managed to maintain his balance for a few seconds before he stumbled into the back of a woman kneeling on the floor with another gang of kids. She looked up at him.

'James?'

James had met Annie while they were getting their degrees in St Patrick's College in Maynooth. She sat beside him in his On Being Christian Together class. They were in the same choir. They went to prayer groups together, mass together. Together they went on retreats and slept in separate beds in old dormitory rooms in monasteries and convents. They confessed one after the other, and they tried their best not to sin, each on their own, and especially not together. Two semesters after they met, they kissed. Four months later he got his hand inside her bra. After a year of sleeping in the same bed, she helped him ejaculate. 'What a mess,' she said. They graduated, and he stayed on at Maynooth for a master's in theology while she signed up for a H.Dip. in education and moved into a small apartment in Drumcondra with two other girls. One Tuesday, he called over for a coffee. 'Can you sit down for a minute?' she said. He hadn't seen her since.

'James?' Annie said again. She was wrinklier, saggier; she looked terrible. For the first time in months he almost smiled. 'How are you? Are you working here!?'

James nodded. Ethel smiled, patted his arm and abandoned him for the other room. He crouched down on his hunkers next to Annie.

'I'm okay,' he said. 'How's things yourself?'

'Well, I'm married! And ...' She reached out and put one hand on each of the two small girls, twins probably, who looked up from their work of smearing paint across squares of cardboard, their own thick hands and arms, and the floor. One was chubby, and a snot trail glistened from her stubby nose down into her open mouth. The other was fatter still and had managed to get chocolate from the bar she was chewing smeared across both her chins. 'This is Hannah, and Holly. They're going to be five next week. Girls, this is James, an old friend of Mommy's.'

The two girls stared at him for a moment then returned to their work, seemingly unimpressed.

'I can't believe you're working here,' said Annie. 'Last I heard you were still in Maynooth doing your Ph.D.'

'Well, after my thesis was rejected I went travelling for a while and came back and did a lot of drinking. Then I had a nervous breakdown. I'm living with my mother now, and her boyfriend. He got me this job.'

'Oh my God. James!'

There was a long moment where they just looked at each other. Then he said, 'Don't worry. I'm fine.'

'Well, it must be nice, working here?'

'Not really.'

'Oh. So have you any other plans?'

'I think I'm going to kill myself.'

Nervous laughter blurted from her open mouth. She gaped down at her daughters, back up at James. She did not ask James why he might want to kill himself, nor did she try to talk him out of it, and it was only now that James realised that he had mentioned suicide to her in the hope that she would say something comforting, that her voice would call out to him from that distant chapter of his life when he was content.

'Do you need any more paint or anything?' He stood up straight and edged his way out through the room's back entrance. He grabbed his satchel from the staff lockers, went to the Gents toilets and locked himself in a cubicle. Pen in hand, he pulled his printed-off letter out of his bag and began to give it its final read-through.

'James?' Derek hit the steering wheel of his Lexus 400 with the palm of his hand. 'I'm talking to you.'

James looked up from his reading. 'What do you want me to do?'

'To have some consideration for your mother's well-being. She's very worried about you.'

'She'll be fine,' said James. 'She's stronger than you think.'

'You mightn't be so sure about that if you were the one she kept awake all night with her tossing and turning.'

'Please don't talk to me about being in bed with my mother.'

Derek steered the car into the right lane of the Stillorgan bypass and surged past a lorry. 'You know she's smoking again?'

A year before that, James was lying under his bed when he heard, from the far side of his stale Phibsboro bedsit, a key in the door. It felt like someone had stuck the key in his ear, and turned it. He opened his eyes and looked at the slats four inches above his face. *What's happening?* he thought. Echoes of his dream came back to him, a nightmare, his mother calling him.

No. His mother was calling him. 'James? James?'

He heard her flat soles slap on the lino of the kitchenette, thud on the bare carpet of the living area, coming closer, bearing down on him. He heard her sigh, hitch up her skirt and lower herself onto her knees. He heard her heavy, uneven breathing, and he turned his head to the left and into the force of her gaze.

'What are you doing under the bed?'

He squeezed his eyes shut, and opened them again. She was still there, still watching him. He squeezed his eyes shut. He heard her sigh, stand up and walk away. The door closed. He couldn't believe she would leave him there like that. He didn't know her at all. The air thickened with silence.

Then she came back. He heard her boil the kettle, pour herself a mug of tea and sit down on the chair next to his bed. She had just gone to the shop, for milk and teabags. A match was struck, the tip of a cigarette fizzed. As far as James knew, she had quit, years ago. The smell of her Silk Cut Purples dragged his childhood forward into his mangy bedsit, and its hope and wonder sat rotting on the air. When she lit her fourth fag he edged his way out from under the bed and pulled himself up onto the mattress. She was sitting there, smoking, looking at him.

'Give me one of those,' he said.

Once James started to write his suicide letter, he was surprised at how much he had to say. He'd spent days, weeks, months sitting in the museum, and lying awake at night, composing sentences in his mind. In the evenings, he would type them up on his iMac and try to arrange them in an order that made sense.

There were several pages on his father's death, when James was twelve, and his mother's subsequent melancholy. There was a long section on the helpless love he had felt for Annie, and the seeping, scabrous wound in his soul that love left behind when she dumped him. He discussed God, the hand at the small of his back that had guided him through his adolescence and on into his college years, and the anxiety he felt when he began to question his faith even as he was reading for his Ph.D. and his terror when, defending his thesis, the external examiner had asked him questions he wasn't prepared for and he realised he no longer believed what he himself had been preaching. Finally, an extensive treatise on the meaninglessness of human existence, with quotes from Nietzsche, E. M. Cioran and Raymond Carver.

It was almost midnight when James finished reading it through and put the pages, all one hundred and seventy-nine of them, in the bin under his desk. In his years in academia he had encountered some pretty solipsistic, obnoxious writing, but this was the worst thing he'd ever read. He knelt on the floor, then lay down. What had he been trying to do? Impress people with his ideas? Get them to pity him? Was he so pathetic he needed others to admire him, or feel sorry for him, even after he was dead? It was hard to believe he had written something so rank with self-importance when the whole point was that nothing was important, least of all his own self.

He crawled up onto his chair, opened the file, selected all and hit delete. Then he typed: Betty, I know this will hurt you. But what's new? All I can do, alive or dead, is bring misery. At least, this way, there will be an end to it, you will get over it. It's harder to get over things that go on living. James.

'James?' Betty knocked again on the door she'd already opened. 'Are you not going to work?'

'I don't feel well.'

She walked into the room and put her hand on his forehead.

'Get off, will you? Let me sleep.'

'I'm going to Superquinn,' she said. 'Can I get you anything?'

He pulled the duvet up over his head. When he heard the front door bang he got up, printed the note, sat down and stared at it. The short paragraph was stranded on the broad A4 sheet. The paper felt cheap in his hand, thin and crinkling beneath the grip of his thumb and finger. The ink was smudged, and the default font of his Mac's word processor seemed trivial. He crumpled it up and threw it in the bin.

He showered and dressed, got the bus into town and spent an hour touring the stationery and art-supply shops on Thomas Street. He bought an elegant, unlined letter pad of thick, water-marked notepaper and spent a week's wages on a Cross fountain pen with a fourteen-carat gold nib and rich, dark-blue ink. He caught another bus back to his mother's house, cleared his desk of the keyboard and other clutter, wiped it clean, washed his hands and tried out his new purchases.

He found it difficult to keep his lines horizontal and evenly spaced; they kept veering up or down as they approached the right-hand margin. His handwriting was sprawling and lop-sided and, he realised, largely illegible. He tried to write slower, taking more care to form the correct shape of each letter. He tried again, and again. Then he threw the pen onto the pile of balled-up paper in his bin.

'James?'

His mother and Derek were sitting on either end of the couch, reading to Schubert's *Wintereisse*. James paused in the doorway, a new top-of-the-range Hewlett-Packard LaserJet printer and a ream of A5, one hundred grams per square metre, Premium Matte Coated paper stacked in his arms.

Betty sat forward on the cushion. 'Don't get mad, sweetheart.'

'What?'

'I called that therapist and made an appointment for you for Tuesday week. Derek says you have that day off.'

James turned away from her and leaned his forehead against the doorframe and closed his eyes. *Actually*, he thought, *that's fine*. He opened them and turned back to his mother.

'Okay,' he said.

'You'll go?'

'Sure. What time is it for?'

'Four o'clock,' said his mother.

'I'll drive you, if you like,' said Derek.

'Great,' said James.

His mother stood and walked across the rug towards him, opening her arms for a hug.

'No need for that, now,' said James.

She stopped and smiled the gentlest, most gormless smile James had ever seen. Standing in the middle of the floor, in her pastel cardigan and wool skirt, her hair caught up in a bun at the top of her head, she looked like an old woman.

'Did you get your hair done?' said James.

She nodded and cupped her bun in her palm. 'Our golf classic is on tomorrow, if you fancy a round? The forecast isn't bad at all.'

'I have to work.'

'Is that a new printer? Did something happen your old one?'

'I needed this for a project I'm working on.'

'That sounds interesting. What sort of project?'

'I should have something to show you soon,' said James.

At three in the morning, James was still experimenting with fonts. Times New Roman was perfectly respectable but seemed a little too formal, too sterile? Garamond had more style, was more bookish than businesslike, but maybe came across as pretentious? Courier was too old-fashioned. Arial was a bore. Helvetica wanted to be cool. Verdana thought it was fun.

He laid copies printed in a range of options out on his bed and stood staring at them.

Betty,

I know this will hurt you. But what's new? All I can do, alive or dead, is bring misery. At least, this way, there will be an end to it, you will get over it. It's harder to get over things that go on living.

James.

Betty,

I know this will hurt you. But what's new? All I can do, alive or dead, is bring misery. At least, this way, there will be an end to it, you will get over it. It's harder to get over things that go on living.

James.

```
Betty,

I know this will hurt you. But what's new? All I
can do, alive or dead, is bring misery. At least,
this way, there will be an end to it, you will
get over it. It's harder to get over things that
go on living.

James.
```

Betty,

I know this will hurt you. But what's new? All I can do, alive or dead, is bring misery. At least, this way, there will be an end to it, you will get over it. It's harder to get over things that go on living.

James.

Betty,

I know this will hurt you. But what's new? All I can do, alive or dead, is bring misery. At least, this way, there will be an end to it, you will get over it. It's harder to get over things that go on living.

James.

Betty,

I know this will hurt you. But what's new? All I can do, alive or dead, is bring misery. At least, this way, there will be an end to it, you will get over it. It's harder to get over things that go on living.

James.

He decided to sleep on it.

'James?'

He opened his eyes and saw Derek silhouetted against the *Rose Nocturne* behind him.

'I'm awake,' he said.

'That's okay,' said Derek. And he stood there. He looked smaller.

'James,' he said. 'I have some terrible news.'

It was a heart attack, on the tenth tee. It was serious. She was in St Vincent's, in intensive care.

They drove there together, Derek's Lexus a hobbled bull staggering through the Friday afternoon traffic. They didn't talk.

Behind the key-coded doors of the ICU the nurse ushered them into an empty waiting room. They were operating. They'd know more in a couple of hours.

Friends and relatives trickled in. With each new arrival, Derek welled up, his voice cracked, and James updated them on the situation.

A heart attack, on the tenth tee. They were operating. They'd know more in a couple of hours.

Everyone said she was going to be fine. Everyone told him how strong she was.

A doctor took James and Derek aside. She had come through the operation. An emergency bypass. She was sleeping now. They'd know more in a couple of hours.

Father Mullins arrived. He'd seen her on the course only last week.

They sat in the packed waiting room and drank tea.

'Maybe an oul prayer,' said Uncle Tommy.

They did a decade.

The priest left.

Friends and relatives trickled in and out.

A heart attack, on the tenth tee. They'd done an emergency bypass. She was sleeping now, they'd know more in a couple of hours.

They talked about the priest, who had seen her on the course only last week, and they laughed.

They sat and drank tea.

'And then I said, "Maybe an oul prayer",' said Uncle Tommy, and they laughed.

'You should go home,' they said to James, 'get some rest.'

'I'm all right here,' he said.

In the morning, James and Derek were let in to see her. She was sleeping, grey-skinned. Derek shook by the side of her bed and sobbed into his cravat. James stood back, at her feet, and looked at the charts, the screens, the tubes pushed up into her arm.

They'd know more in a couple of hours.

Friends and relatives trickled in and out.

They talked about the priest, and they laughed.

A heart attack on the tenth tee.

It was serious.

'She's awake,' said the doctor to James and Derek. 'You can have five minutes. She's still very sick.'

Inside, James moved around the bed, crept closer to her grey-skinned face. He held her hand, and she squeezed his finger.

'Hi Mam,' he said.

'I was three under after nine,' she said.

Two hours later, she died.

James and Derek sat in the back of the funeral director's black Mercedes, the second car in the procession from the Foxrock funeral home to the church in Rathcoole.

'Jessica said I can move into the spare room in her house in Rathmines,' said James.

'Your cousin?'

James nodded.

'You want to move out?'

'I figure you don't really want to see me around all the time.'

'Well,' said Derek. 'There's no sense in pointing fingers now.'

The driver steered them around another roundabout.

'If that's what you want, that's fine,' said Derek, 'but there's no hurry. I think I'll take a few weeks away, soon, maybe go and see my sister and her family in Atlanta.'

'That sounds nice,' said James.

Derek looked at him. He seemed a different person in his white shirt and sober black tie. 'Are you going to stay on at the museum?'

'For a while anyway,' said James. 'I'll have to find something else to do eventually, but …' He shrugged. 'I suppose we'll see what happens.'

From his attic room, James heard the front door open and close, and Derek's Lexus start up, turn and purr down the driveway. He opened his desk drawer and pulled out the printed copies of his suicide letter. He took his bin, with the long version and dozens of crumpled attempts at the pithy one, and the remainder of the ream of A5 paper, and he walked down through the house and out into the back garden.

He lit a fag, pulled back a garden chair and sat down. It was a cold December night, and the light from above the back door struggled to reach him through the foggy darkness. He held his note in the air, the paper's premium matte coating a dull grey against the tall black Cypress trees that bordered the lawn. Then he sparked his lighter and held it to the bottom right corner of the letter. Flames bounced and receded as an orange arc smouldered its way across the page. The flames reached his fingertips and he dropped the last corner of the note on the damp grass. Breathing the acrid air, he raised another copy in the air and sparked his lighter again. He burned each variation like that, then every page from the bin, then the blank sheets from the ream, and its paper wrapping.

★

James sat staring at the *Rose Nocturne*. Its waves seemed redder today, less pink. Perhaps, he thought, it was something to do with the light. A phone rang in his trousers, and he rooted in his pocket, confused because he thought he'd put his on silent and left it in his locker, and because the ringtone was wrong. The scattering of tourists and retirees wandering the room turned to stare at him. Just as his hand found the phone he remembered it was his mother's.

'Hello?' he said. It was a lady from Dr Jenkins' office, calling because a James Clancy had not shown up for his appointment at four o'clock. James apologised, said there had been a misunderstanding.

'Would you like to reschedule the appointment?'

'No, that's okay,' said James. 'He's all right now. He's going to be fine.'

QUALITY TIME

MADELEINE D'ARCY

I f only one of those idiot nurses would turn his television on. All he had to contemplate was the ceiling above him. That dreadful ceiling, with its banal magnolia paint. Supreme blandness, but for a daub in a slightly darker shade right above his bed. An oddly shaped imperfection – the result, he was convinced, of something more sinister – blood from an exploding vein, a leaping spurt of pus, an ejaculation? The reason for the overlay of paint obsessed him daily since he'd found himself stretched out on this hospital bed, helpless and utterly immobile.

The multiple ignominies of the past week made him seethe with impotent fury, but at least the lackeys had not overlooked his Laya GoldPlus health insurance, so he had a private room. His field of vision was limited to the upper part of the door on his left and of the window on the right, that dratted ceiling, the helpless emergency cord dangling like a neglected toy barely visible in the corner of his eye and, thankfully, the television, hanging on its metal limb high up on the far wall.

On duty today was the one he called Nurse Wretched. If only he could speak, he'd have a thing or two to say to that bitch. He detested all the nurses, in fact, except for little Nursie Tinybones, with her soft plump hands and incongruous scent of bubblegum and flowers. And Patchett, the physio, was not a bad sort – at least she provided the only smidgen of bodily ease he'd experienced since that blasted stroke.

If only bloody Nurse Wretched would switch the dratted TV on. The careless cow had also left his door ajar. He could hear the enervating clatter of the underlings outside and smell some disastrous boiled vegetableness floating in the disinfectant air. Even more excruciating was Wretched's fake-sincere chatter with some female in the corridor outside.

'So, here he is, and won't he be delighted to see you, the poor poppet!' Nurse Wretched squealed as she swung round the door and into the room, hovering over him, showing him off as if he were Exhibit A.

'Now, look who's come all the way from London to see her dear old dad!' she cooed.

If only Wretched would drop dead.

'Thank you, nurse.' The other woman's voice seemed unaccountably familiar, despite the slight English accent.

'He can't turn his head, dear. You'll have to get in close so he'll see you.'

A middle-aged woman leaned over him. There was something distinctly recognisable about her.

'So … this is a Diving Bell and Butterfly scenario, is it?' asked the woman in her Englishy accent.

'What?'

'Am I correct to assume that he knows what's going on even though he can't move or speak or … well, do anything?'

'He can move his eyes, dear, but that's all. That's how we know he likes to watch the telly.'

The Englishwoman looked at him, and he rolled both his eyes at her.

There, he thought. *See what you make of that, girlie. See what you make of that.*

'And all these tubes?'

'Well, pet, he can't breathe properly without them. We have to feed him intravenously as well.' Nurse Wretched lowered her voice. 'He has to wear an incontinence pad down below, of course.'

'And you don't know how long this condition will last?'

'No, dear … well, I'm not allowed to say. You'll have to talk to the Consultant.'

'I understand. Thank you, nurse.'

'Right, then. I'll leave you to it.'

Exit Nurse Wretched. The door clunked shut behind her.

The Englishwoman leaned over, so that he could see her face again.

'Well, well, Dad,' she said. 'Long time, no see. It's me, Trisha.'

Yes, it was his daughter, Trisha. He recognised those bitter little eyes, the bone structure of her face, the still-beautiful hair. She must be almost forty now, he supposed. Well preserved, all the same. The lovely smooth blonde hair – a shame she wore it shorter now – what was the name of that style? A bob? The outfit was pitiful, somewhat like the clothes that Wifey used to wear. A blue denim jacket over a white blouse. Did they still call them blouses? Cheap dangly earrings. No class. How could she? Wifey had no class either. In the end, he had despised Wifey. Though not as much as she despised him, he supposed. He blinked. I'm still here girlie. See what you make of that.

Trisha looked almost afraid, but she recovered within moments. 'You're in there all right, aren't you? You're still there, Dad. Not that you deserve to be.'

The colour of his daughter's hair was darker than he recalled. Ash blonde, was it? In his memory, she was a fairytale child with long golden tresses. From this rancid bedtrap he could still imagine – almost feel – the smooth ripeness of her hair.

'Trust you to have great health insurance. Just as well, I suppose. You're going to be here for a long time.' She walked around the bed, and from the other side she leaned over again to peer into his face.

'Can you hear me?' she asked, loudly. She looked into his eyes. 'You're in there all right, you bastard. Yes, it's me, your daughter. Let's spend some quality time together, shall we?' She straightened up and walked back around the bed. She sat down in the chair. He could barely see her now, but he could smell a faint lemony perfume.

'Hilarious that you can't talk,' she said, in a hard voice. 'You used to have plenty to say, didn't you? Hardly ever stopped ranting at Mum and upsetting her. When you were in the house, the only time we had peace was when you read to me. But the books you chose – I couldn't understand half of them. Remember *Don Quixote*? Tilting at windmills. I had no idea what it was all about. I was probably only four then. I just listened. I'd do anything to keep you in a good mood.'

He remembered, quite suddenly and clearly, the cover of that book: a daft old man on a horse, wearing yellow armour, and little Sancho Panza, his underling, bound to obey a lunatic who was out of control. The tale had amused him once.

'I remember the way you brushed my hair and counted. Forty slow brushstrokes on each section, and then you'd ... oh God ...' She put her head in her hands.

He thought she might be crying. What the heck was she fussing about?

'I wish Mum could see you now – the state of you – but she can't. She's dead. She died two years ago. Did you know that? I didn't bother letting you know. If only she had had your medical insurance – but the NHS wasn't too bad.' She wiped her eyes.

He heard the door open. Nurse Minnie Mouse squeaked in, all pert and businessy as usual.

'Just got to do his bloods,' she chirped.

How he hated them all.

At his side he felt, rather than saw, Trisha rising from the chair.

'No need to move,' Nurse Minnie Mouse said. 'You can stay if you like. So long as you're not squeamish.'

'No, I'm not a bit squeamish. Thank you, nurse.'

He felt her sit down again, a small flow of air and that lemon fragrance, with a hint of flowers, perhaps lilies.

'You're the daughter, aren't you? Call me Barbara,' Mousey said cheerfully, as she jabbed a needle most painfully into the flesh of his upper arm. How he longed to roar at that despicable woman. All her persnickety tidiness and yet she was clueless about the most basic of tasks. That small rodent face of hers was asking to be hit.

'I hear you only just arrived from London,' said Mousey to his daughter. 'You must be exhausted. I could bring you a cup of tea, if you like?'

'That's very kind of you, but I'm fine, thanks.'

'So, whereabouts in London do you live?'

He wished Mousey would quit sticking her nosy little nose in. He hated her even more than Nurse Wretched now.

'Muswell Hill.'

'That's North London, isn't it? I used to live in Clapham once upon a time.'

'I lived there too, for a while, when I was ten. Then my mother met my stepfather, so we moved to North London when I was twelve.'

From his stodgy static bed he felt intensely vexed. *So Wifey had met someone else, the bitch? Surely it couldn't have lasted.*

'And do you come back to Ireland very often?'

'Not really,' said Trisha.

'Well, at least you're here now, that's the main thing, isn't it?' Nurse Minnie Mouse squeaked.

He could not see what the nurse was doing, but he could hear her fannying about beside him, probably fixing adhesive labels on the vials of his still-warm blood.

'Yes,' said his daughter, absently.

The nurse fumbled at the bottom of the bed. She wrote on a chart with a blue biro before returning the pen to her breast pocket and replacing the chart.

'All done for now,' she said. 'I'll leave you in peace.' Exit Nurse Minnie Mouse with a see-through envelope containing his blood.

As soon as the door closed, Trisha spoke again. 'She's left us in peace, Dad,' she said. 'Pity you never left us in peace.' She stood up and began to pace. 'Mum was never right afterwards, you know. She tried. God help her, she tried. But she always went for the wrong men.'

Wifey was an idiot. That had become obvious over time. He could not conceive now of any possible reason why he had ever married Wifey, but it was hardly his fault she was an idiot.

'Mum was so naive,' his daugher continued. 'Of course, people didn't talk about things in those days.' There she was again, at the side of the bed. She leaned over and stared into his eyes. 'Can you hear me? Yes, you can, can't you? So, let's see, how many years is it since we had some quality time together? Thirty, maybe? Can you cast your mind back?'

How sarcastic she was, the little bitch.

'Of course, Mum should have faced up to things, but she didn't. You got off scot-free. You probably went on doing the same kind of thing all your life. Men like you, they don't stop, do they?'

A phone rang out, a cheerful cha cha cha tone.

'Hang on.' She reached down, and he could hear a zip being unzipped, some fumbling sounds. She stood up and plonked her handbag on the bed. 'Yes, that's fine. I'll be there,' she said, into one of those new-fangled phones, before replacing it in the bag. She took out a handkerchief and blew her nose, before continuing. 'Poor Mum. I blamed her for a long time, you know. She was so naive. In spite of those enormous blue eyes she couldn't see what was going on under her nose.'

She got up again and began to pace up and down. 'I wanted to tell her for so long, but you wouldn't let me. You said I could never tell. You used to stroke my hair. Remember? You washed my hair too. That was one of your jobs. Then you'd plait it.'

Ah, yes, he had loved every hair on her little urchin head. He used to brush it for hours and smooth it into two beautiful princess-like ponytails or plait it in various delightful ways. He could almost feel the sap rising now. How delicious it was when her little friends began to ask him to arrange their hair too, to fix it in pretty plaits like hers. Perhaps he should have been a hairdresser. In his day, only women did that job. It was a sissy job, though, and he was certainly never a sissy.

'My friends all wanted plaits like mine. Mary Kate came to our house, one day, to play. You came home early from work, remember? Mum said, "Great, you're back early. I'll just pop out to the butcher's." You plaited Mary Kate's hair, and then she went home, and then you took down my hair and brushed it straight, and you said my hair was the prettiest and that you loved me more than you loved anyone and that we had to be nice to each other. You said it was our secret. You'd have to cut my beautiful hair off if I told, and I'd have no hair left, and I'd be ugly, and I'd look like a boy, and that would be horrible.'

She sounded almost out of breath as she paced around the

room. He couldn't see much of her, but he could feel a minuscule flow of air as she moved back and forth somewhere near the foot of his bed. Maybe she was waving her arms. A windmill daughter. Or maybe a Don Quixote daughter, tilting uselessly at windmills. Once upon a time, she had sat on his knee while he read that book aloud. She was too young to understand the story, but he read it to her anyway.

'The shock of it. I can't describe it. Seeing my friend, Mary Kate, with her hair shorn. Stubby little haircut, like a boy's. The look on her face. "I'm never going to your house again," she said. "I can't be your friend any more." I knew it was your fault, but I said nothing. You cut my hair off anyway, in the end.'

He remembered that little spoilsport, Mary Kate, who had told her mother about the fun they'd had. The little brat. She had had the most delicious chestnut hair. She told her story once, but she refused to tell it again, because he'd warned her, you see. Hair first, neck next, he'd whispered in her tiny ear. Ah, the overwhelming pleasure of that thick rope of hair shifting in his hand. Oh, the sheer joy of the blades working through the sheaf of chestnut brown. No choice but to do it once again, with his own, the blonde.

'What did you do to her? What other awful things did you do?' She leaned over him and stared right into his eyes. 'How could you live with yourself? I can hardly live with myself, and I did nothing wrong. You bastard.'

She moved out of his view again and paced while she spoke. 'You know what, I was jealous. Can you believe it? You always said you loved me the most, and then I found out you were doing the same things with Mary Kate. Crazy, isn't it? But that's the way it was.'

She stopped and faced the window. Her smooth blonde hair touched the collar of her blue denim jacket. Shame it was so short now. 'We were lucky. We got help in London,' she told the window. 'A great charity. I still donate. Only for that place we'd have been on the streets. The thing is, I've had therapy since then – loads of therapy – but I can't get over it.' She paused and took a deep breath. 'I still feel guilty,' she continued. 'We just ran away. We left you there to do as you pleased. That didn't solve anything. For men like you, there's only one solution.'

He heard her unzip her bag again. There was a metallic swishing sound. 'See what I have?' she said, towering over him now with a large chrome scissors in her hand. 'Chop chop.' She snipped the scissors open, closed, open, closed, right in front of his face.

'How do you like this?' she said. 'All these tubes. I could snip them all.'

Finally, he was afraid. It would be a painful death. Such hatred in her eyes. As usual, no Wretched Nursie, no Minnie Mousey Nursie, no little Nursie Tinybones. Like buses, there was not a single bloody nursie around when you needed one.

He felt cold air on his lower body. She had raised the bed-clothes. He could only imagine the pathetic sight: his bare old legs, the hospital nightdress, the bulge of his hospital diapers underneath. His warm urine flowed along a catheter, and there was an itch somewhere on his left foot that he would never be able to scratch.

'I think I'll take your nappy off and give you a snip,' she said. 'I could do a right job on you, couldn't I? I could snip, snip, snip your dirty great thing right off.'

He felt the bedclothes being replaced carefully.

'Hmm,' she said and leaned over. She snipped the scissors several times, efficiently, in front of his face. Then she stopped and looked straight into his eyes. 'Not today,' she sighed. 'I can't be bothered today. Snip snip. I'll take my time about it. See you tomorrow.'

She picked up her handbag and held it high, so he could see her place the scissors carefully inside. 'Toodle-pip and toodle-oo,' she called, as she left the room.

Damn it, he thought, his heart racing. He had once accused Wifey of having a fancy man. He'd even tried to slap the truth out of her. He'd been certain the child was not his own. Now, he realised he had been wrong. This girl was flesh of his flesh, blood of his blood. The same feisty spirit. That zest for danger. The delicious tension. The tantalising feeling that a nurse could walk in on them at any moment. What a cunning little vixen. He was almost looking forward to her next visit.

But now the television was blank. That blasted Nurse Wretched. He wished she'd hurry up and turn it on.

THE LATE BITE

GINA MOXLEY

His days followed much the same pattern – the newspaper, the radio, a doze – though slower, much, much slower than before. And the weeks were punctuated by his children dropping by, all four of them, according to some rota they devised themselves which was meant to seem random rather than planned. He wasn't up to going to them any more, which was handy since he'd lost interest in their labyrinthine lives. The couch was now in the kitchen, saving him the shuffle from place to place. It was firm without being uncomfortable, and he was thankful for its solid, collegial support. The television, microwave, phone, were all within reach, while disease made free with his bones. He was eighty-five. His pills were laid out like septuplets, in separate baby-pink cots, a mournful black capital indicating the day on the lid of the box. These were a new set of tablets, for pain management rather than any hope of a restoration to full health, the final furlong of the grind to a halt. He'd been to see the consultant on Tuesday, when he was told the prognosis was not great.

'Doc,' he had said, irked. 'Don't beat around the bush. I'd appreciate if you'd give it to me straight.'

He was a man who felt he could cope with almost anything if he was given the chance to prepare. As a teenager, he had spent a few years in the army, where he learnt that if he was to get anywhere, planning was key. From there, he lifted himself by the bootstraps and charted a path: he would become an apprentice to a printer, learn the trade, with the eventual goal of owning his own business. His approach had to be methodical, there were no handouts – his own father had died when he was three, leaving a large family. There was no money for university, everything would be achieved through hard graft. Once he was able to provide for a family he would get married. And his stolid groundwork had served him well. His life went according to plan. Without hitch or surprise. Until Hilary died. He was totally unprepared. A massive coronary, and out she went, without warning, like a light in the night. The shock of waking to his wife beside him, yellowing and marble cold, unravelled his military training. The spate of his loss ran unchecked for days; the pivot of his life was gone.

'Please,' he continued, his tone less gruff. 'No pussyfooting. I'd like to know what to expect.'

A past master of difficult situations, the consultant looked at him evenly. He knew that the return to dust was well under way beneath his patient's clothes. They both did. It just needed confirmation. The old man's two daughters had come with him, and one had brought her son. The women held hands. His sons were caught up with work.

'Six months.'

The sentence slammed home like a gavel hitting the block. Finality hung in the air. The old man nodded his thanks. Right, he thought, six multiplied by four multiplied by seven gives one hundred and sixty-eight days to go. He was a literal man and expected to live it out to the date. The daughters and child fell asunder – Oh Dad, oh Daddy, oh Granddad – untrammelled already by grief, when all he wanted was to be left alone. After the what ifs and the maybes, there was some talk of what would happen next, both of his girls offering to take him to theirs for the stretch. But the very idea of it, all that noise, constant food and computers, was too much for him to bear.

'Stop,' he said, rather sharply. ' Let's see how I fare.'

At the shopping centre, his eldest girl, Elaine, went to pick up the new prescription, while the other, Alison, went to do a big food shop – they never stopped buying, those daughters of his, accumulating more and more stuff when they already had so much. He waited in the car, cold though the sun shone outside, pinging off windscreens in the car park. A draught licked his nape where the collar was too big for his neck. He rummaged in the pocket of his fleece jacket, then gave his grandson some money and asked him to go buy him a wall calendar, big print, yes, one with separate days. Finally alone with his sentence, he uttered, 'I'm going to die,' with palliative calm. He said it again, his voice unwavering, and braced himself, expecting some torrent of feeling to ambush him. His milky eyes looked around to check. A sniper of sadness. Or fear. But no, nothing came. Not relief. Nor longing. Nor a god luring him with promises of a heavenly renewal of vows. His burst of anguish – mortifying in retrospect – after Hilary went, had cauterised the emotional part of his brain. A portcullis came down. For the past eight years there had been no highs or lows, he ploughed, head bowed, across the prairie of some abstract terrain. Earlier that summer, when he first became ill, he went to see his solicitor to make sure his affairs were in order. Now all the paperwork was up to date, the will was made – everything divided equally between the four children, no favourites. His work was done, the day had been named. He was prepared.

His grandson returned, proudly waving his purchase, neatly rolled up in a tube. Since it was August, an academic year planner was all there was to be had. That suited just nicely, no pictures of animals or water lilies to distract, and it ran well into the next year. With several months to spare.

'Good lad, keep the change.'

Right at that minute, he couldn't remember the child's name.

★

In the kitchen, Elaine and Alison unpacked bags and bags of shopping while he sat silently on the couch. As if food would lessen the blow. He wouldn't have to shop again until he died. The sight of it made him weary, he strained to stop nodding off. It had been an eventful day.

'We should ring Paddy. I told him I would.'

'Text him. He'll still be in surgery.'

Alison frowned at her sister. It wasn't the type of information to send by text. Their father caught the look.

'Dad, would you like to speak to him?' Alison asked.

Her father shook his head. Paddy was a dentist, the first to go to university; he didn't want to interrupt his son's work. There really was no urgency, he had six months, why the fuss? Then Elaine said, 'Who's going to break it to Dennis? He's in London all this week. He'll be in bits, being away.'

'Ring Sheila,' Alison suggested. Neither of the girls was that keen on their brother's wife.

'Oh, the lady of leisure,' sneered Elaine. 'She'll probably be out golfing. In fairness, she does little else. No, you ring her.'

'Okay!'

He wished they would just go. At his grandfather's request, Rory – his name came back from the blue – pinned the calendar to the wall, over the table, in full view. The daughters glanced at each other awkwardly as they watched their father count out the days of his damning decree. Taking a marker, he drew a diagonal line through Tuesday, 21 August, and said, 'One down,' though the day wasn't over yet.

'Ah, Dad,' Alison said. 'Don't.' A shellac of saliva coated her words.

Sniffling, Elaine took a sweeping brush to the frill of fluff that fringed the room.

'Sorry,' their father apologised, half-heartedly. His girls were neurotic about dust. 'I haven't been able.'

Alison stood facing him, trying not to look at him, to watch him whittle away. Instead, the ormolu clock on the shelf above him snared her attention.

'I love that old thing,' she gulped, swallowing the lump in her throat, nodding up at the clock. What she wanted to do was hug her dad, throw her arms around him, to hold his crumbling frame, to whisper some consolation, but she knew his hands would fly up like a preacher keeping any intimacy at bay.

'Well, take it with you. It's only gathering dust up there.'

'Ah, Dad,' Alison protested, eyes brimming. 'I didn't mean it like that. No. I don't want it. I was just at a loss for something to say.'

'Take it,' he insisted, in a voice riddled with rust. 'Where I'm going, what need will I have for time? I don't even wind it; the tick is too loud.'

Glaring, Elaine sidled up to her sibling. 'That was meant to be mine.'

Then a bushfire of tiredness swept through him, his head dipped, and he burnt out like a match. While he dozed, Alison and Elaine erupted into a whirlwind of cleaning armed with a blizzard of sprays. The grandchild watched cartoons on TV.

Day three of one-sixty-eight.

'What was that noise?' he wondered, on the second morning he woke alive. The third day of the countdown. Unaccounted-for sounds unnerved him; they spelt trouble, like burglars or leaks. He was standing at the kitchen counter, having popped the lid of his T for Thursday pillbox. He had washed, dressed and was feeling quite chipper. And there it was again: tap tap tap.

'Bloody hell, it's the front door.'

The bell was broken. The children all used the back entrance, and anyone he knew either didn't call any more or was dead. He implored that it wasn't his neighbour, Eileen Creed. He had danced with her at some wedding, a year or so after Hilary died. She nauseated him with her coquettish flirting and her sly 'There's still life in the old dog though.' Occasionally, she would come to the door with a casserole, letting on she'd made too much for one and it would only go off. He refused all her offers of dinners, not wanting anything of her on his table, not to mention letting her inside. She had knocked again some time recently, when word of his illness first went out. Realising it was she – he heard her speak to the postman outside – he decided not to answer.

'He must be dead,' she had squawked, causing a commotion.

Somebody then called an ambulance, and all the palaver that ensued. That was when? June. About two and a half months ago. Four plus four plus two equals ten, multiplied by seven gives seventy. Seventy days ago, approximately. Time flew. He had since given her a wide berth. Sirens and hysteria were the last thing he needed, so he decided to brave it, and slowly he made his way to the door thinking, 'To hell with her and her stew.'

'Hello, Mr Holmes,' said the man standing there. A man in his mid-thirties. Rough around the edges. Cheap clothes. Some scars. But the eyes …

'Yes,' Mr Holmes said in acknowledgement. Those eyes were unmistakable – cobalt blue. Then he continued, 'Jimmy James?'

This visitor was most unexpected. He had resigned himself to never laying eyes on him again.

'The very same,' Jimmy nodded, confirming his old pet name.

Mr Holmes had to lean against the hall table in case he slithered like a silk slip to the floor.

'Long time.'

'Long time.'

Warmly and firmly they shook hands, with neither breaking away. They went inside to the kitchen and each took a chair. Last time they had seen each other was when Mr Holmes visited Jimmy in London, Pentonville Prison, a dozen years before. The only contact since had been the birthday cards that Jimmy had sent him, year in and year out, arriving bang on the day. No news, updates or return address, just 'From Jimmy, with all my best' in that loopy, sloping scrawl. They sat for a while, wondering where to begin.

'Hilary died eight years ago. In '99. Not long after I retired.'

Jimmy shook his head. 'I'm sorry to hear it. Really sorry. I didn't know.'

Hilary had been fond of Jimmy initially, but when, after his mother died, he took to the drink, left school and got into trouble with the guards – petty stuff but enough to get a name – her patience waned. He was biting the hand that fed him. She told him out straight. Nothing would do Jimmy but to head off to England; he had cousins there. Mr Holmes did his best to stop him, he offered him a proper job, an apprenticeship, but he didn't want to stay. Instead, he gave Jimmy a couple of hundred pounds on the sly to set himself up while he looked for work. Once he had left for London, he rarely entered Hilary's mind. She didn't accompany her husband when he went to the jail to visit, though she did send a present. A jumper, or was it a book? Another detail lost in the mist of time.

'If I'd known how to get in touch …' Mr Holmes stopped himself, he hadn't meant it to sound like a scold. Jimmy stood. He seemed edgy; the twinkle was gone from his eyes. 'Yeah. Well, I was always moving around. Know what I mean, Mr Holmes? No fixed abode.'

Mr Holmes wondered whether he meant he had been home-less. A down-and-out. That the boy once brimful of potential had been sleeping rough.

'I've let too much sh- … stuff slide.'

He asked Jimmy to put on the kettle, and they fell into the old pattern of the man instructing the boy. Cups, milk, sugar, tea. Spoons over there. Like it was when he first came to the printworks.

Jimmy must have been around ten. His mother, Cathleen, had started as the cleaner; there was no father on the scene. She never whinged or made excuses, though it must have been a struggle to make ends meet. She was smart, but life had dealt her a raw deal. Mr Holmes saw her potential and gradually trained her up in accounts so that she would help him do the wages every week. That year, 1981 or '82, Jimmy came with her during school holidays – the aunt who looked after him was away. On his first day, he brought them tea in the office, unbid-den, the tray laden with clattering cups.

'Two sugars for you, boss. Have you any jobs for me? Come on, boss, give me something to do. You don't even have to pay.' He had the confidence of a rogue.

Initially, Mr Holmes put him with the girls at the table col-lating the sections of books: a simple job, putting the pages in order. Jimmy picked it up easily – the girls mothered him to within an inch of his life – but his attention strayed, he had too much energy to spare. Whenever he saw Mr Holmes at the guillotine he would go and join him, busying himself sweeping up the offcuts. He was a self-starter, a quality his boss admired.

'Steer clear of this monster if you value your fingers,' Mr Holmes warned, as the blade sliced through reams of paper, shearing it into quires. He wiggled the stumps of own index fingers. It was an occupational hazard; he had lopped them off in separate incidents years before. 'You might need them to pick your nose from time to time.'

Jimmy gave a funny hiccupy laugh, and Mr Holmes realised that it wasn't just the machine that interested the boy; rather, he needed responsibility and the company of men. The boss knew this from his own childhood without a father. So, he introduced him to Ambrose, who ran the darkroom, who showed him how to wash the used silk screens, how to hose every trace of the photographic film from the mesh in a special bath. Jimmy was in his element and worked harder than men twice his age. Even the men running the litho machines on the factory floor took to him – an achievement in itself. He became their mascot. And at the end of the week, he got his own brown envelope of cash, his name typed on the front: Jimmy James.

When his mother went into hospital the following summer – some female problem, nobody liked to ask – Mr Holmes took Jimmy to his house to stay. He had presented Hilary with a fait accompli. Where else could the child go? Their own children were reared, Paddy was qualified, Elaine was married. There was plenty of space. She couldn't say no. And she didn't; she understood that her husband wanted to give this boy a chance.

'And I'm on my way out, according to the top man, off to meet my maker,' Mr Holmes said, almost proudly, pointing to the tablets. Then, tapping the asterisk on 5 February on the calendar, continued, 'a hundred and sixty-six days to go.'

Buckled by sudden sadness, Jimmy simply said, 'Oh.'

They drank their tea and had biscuits from the stock the daughters had bought. Mr Holmes took his first daily dose of pills.

'Any tomatoes or cucumbers? Or is it too soon?' Jimmy enquired with forced excitement, deliberately changing tack.

'Ah,' the old man said, with a wave of his hand, 'the glasshouse blew down.'

He was embarrassed by the state of the garden; what was once a model of precision was now ragged and overgrown. He could hardly bear to look out at it any more. He continued, 'Do you remember? You hounded me round that garden, like a pup at my heel. We had it shipshape between us. And you, eating all around you. Do you remember, throwing up that time? The tomatoes were green.'

Jimmy's smile turned into a crumple. 'I sure do, boss. Sure do.'

'Long time ago.'

'And what about the factory?'

'Sold. I thought Dennis might have some interest, but, no.'

At one point, Mr Holmes had hoped he might be able to guide Jimmy, and eventually hand it on to him. But that dream went awry. There was never a chance that Dennis would step in, too educated to get his hands dirty. He wasn't a grafter, not like his old man.

'It must've been hard to see it go.'

'It was,' Mr Holmes said, and shrugged. He had hung on for as long as he could. The family plagued him to retire. Then, when he did, and Hilary died, he was left with nothing to occupy him. Marooned. He didn't want to go over that ground again.

'Is there a girl?' he enquired.

Jimmy laughed, 'I'm a man. What more can I say.'

'So nobody special?' Mr Holmes prodded, without hiding the disappointment in his voice. He wanted him to have an anchor in his life, somebody to moor him, to see his worth.

Jimmy took his time answering; his eyes didn't lift from the floor. Yes, there had been a woman. Between them they had had a little girl, but things took a bad turn. There was no explanation why. He went under. Hit rock bottom. He hadn't been allowed access for years. 'The fall out of love, boss. I tell you, it's dog rough.' The tumble could be heard in his words.

'I'm sorry, Jim,' Mr Holmes said, squeezing the younger man's hand. 'You deserved better than that.' All the preparation in the world couldn't protect a man from that sort of knock.

Jimmy got up and rinsed out their cups. He flicked on the kettle and refilled the milk jug. It reminded Mr Holmes of how easily he got the hang of things. How could he not have luck?

'And work?'

Jimmy raked his hands through his hair. 'Ah, ducking and diving … labouring … landscaping …'

'Is that where you got the scars, pruning roses?' Mr Holmes asked, deliberately trying to lighten the mood. Not wanting to revisit his catalogue of drink, drugs and hard luck, Jimmy acted like he hadn't heard. 'A bit of security. Whatever I could pick up. But now I've decided to come back. Home. It's time to get myself back on the road. A clean start.'

As Jimmy made fresh tea, Mr Holmes wondered what could have prompted his return, whether he was on the run from something. He didn't seem to have picked up any skills. He was certainly broke. 'I could give you a dig out. Until you set yourself up.'

'Stop it now, boss. Please. Don't embarrass me,' Jimmy said with sudden force. 'That's why I came to see you. I still owe you from before.' Back when he first left for London, he would only accept the money Mr Holmes had given him if it was a loan. He'd pay him back. He swore. But no roll of notes appeared from his pocket. Instead, he poured the tea and sat back down. Mr Holmes was suddenly skewered by exhaustion. He wasn't used to company, having to make conversation, and this was like joining the dots. When his children came, they didn't say much. It was all part of a pattern. They asked how he was, and he'd answer, 'Hanging in there.' And that would be that. There might be some mention of what was in the newspaper, something to do with one of their children, and then they'd turn on the television or do some jobs around the house. All of this talking and remembering had worn him out. Though he would normally sleep on the couch, right now he longed for his bed.

'Would you mind if I went up for a doze? I'm in what used to be your room now, away from the noise of the road.'

Jimmy helped him up the stairs and into the boxroom. It still smelled of talcum powder and musty potpourri, but it seemed smaller than before. When he stayed there that summer, Jimmy claimed that he couldn't sleep with the door closed. He had never heard anything like Mr Holmes snoring. He used to lie in bed laughing to himself at it. A big ruffle of a sound that he repeated to general amusement on the factory floor.

'I'll hang on till you wake,' Jimmy said, as he sat the old man down on the bed. He slipped off his shoes for him and covered him with the duvet, like a child.

'Look,' Mr Holmes said, and pointed to a glass marble wedged into a knot in the floorboards.

'Still there,' Jimmy said, laughing, remembering his struggle to shove it in, hammering it down with his shoe.

'Yes,' Mr Holmes said, and smiled.

Jimmy left the door ajar.

In the seconds before sleep, the old man made some decisions. He would change his will, sort Jimmy out, finish what he set out to do by giving him a late bite of the cherry. He would phone the solicitor tomorrow. Yes. Go into town himself if necessary.

Mr Holmes then drifted off to the hoarse haaw of Jimmy pushing and pulling the lawnmower outside.

HEROES

SHEILA LLEWELLYN

oscow, December 1998. I walk out of the Metro station, and Tanya is there to meet me. She looks as elegant as ever, fur-trimmed shapka at a slight angle on her head, the sparkly pin at the side catching the weak winter sunlight. We hug, then start to pick our way through the fresh snowfall along a short strip of road. A sub-zero wind needles my nose and makes my sinuses throb.

Tanya's flat is on the tenth floor of a fifteen-storey block from the Khrushchev era, in a run-down district of South Moscow. Two blocks stand either side of the road connecting the station to the flats. And that's it. Accommodation at one end, efficient transport to work at the other. The old Soviet way: maybe no worse than the West, just stripped down to the essentials.

'Say what you like about the Russians, everyone has a job and a roof over their heads.' My uncle's voice. He's just said this to my father. They're both long dead, but since I came to Russia two months ago, they've been with me, taking turns to tweak my memory. This time, it's 1960, and I'm twelve, sitting between them on my uncle's sofa, watching newsreels of the May Day parade from Red Square. They trade the usual arguments – my uncle, a socialist, veteran of the thirties hunger marches, Manchester Area Secretary of his trade union, and my father, who left fifties Britain behind, made good in the West Indies and has no truck with politics.

Their spat about the Russians is shorter than usual. My father would rather talk about organising my schooling. He's going to do the unthinkable – he's sending me back home. I'll be boarding at a school close enough to stay weekends with my aunt and uncle. The arrangement suits everyone but me. I'm angry with my father, and I'm miserable. It's been just the two of us for as long as I can remember. I've never been without him.

While they're sorting things out, I watch the parade. Children, athletes, ordinary Russian people, all carrying flowers and giant-sized paper doves. Over the black-and-white footage, a BBC voice is saying that this year the Soviets are showing they want peace. Then they show shots of last year's 1959 parade. Endless blocks of soldiers and sailors marching with a pointy-toed hint of a goose-step, followed by tanks and rows of rocket-launchers dwarfing the people. The missiles come last: fat ones, sleek ones, rolling on and on. 'That's the real Soviet Union,' says my father.

My uncle turns the sound down.

Tanya and I pass a few babushki – it's Saturday, so they're out selling eggs and undefinable meat displayed on planks placed across upended plastic crates. Kiosks are also open for bread, alcohol, cigarettes. Tanya stops to buy rye bread, and she and the babushka mutter about the price.

'They won't be around much longer, our babushki,' says Tanya, nodding towards the Universam supermarket near the flats. Once state-controlled, it's just been privatised by the Russian equivalent of Tesco. Economics, or mafia muscle, will force the babushki out of business.

The smell of male sweat, lavender air freshener and stale tobacco hangs about the lift doors of Tanya's block. Graffiti on the walls praises 'Metallica' and suggests we 'fuck off'. I express surprise that 'fuck off' is written in English, and Tanya says our British Council initiative of providing free English lessons to young Russians is obviously a success.

The lift groans but it works and lugs us to the tenth floor. Tanya's mother, Julka, opens the door, and I glimpse Olga, Tanya's daughter, flitting across the tiny hallway in a pink Adidas tracksuit. Julka insists on showing me round before we have lunch. The flat is small but has three rooms, a luxury, but Julka's husband, dead ten years, was a senior engineer and a solid Party man. She's proud of the view from the living-room window. The tiny patch of land below, she assures me, is green under the snow. In the centre is a pond, frozen over. Two small boys are using an old tyre as an ice toboggan, harnessing themselves to it with a red plastic rope and squealing as they pull each other across.

Tanya comes back into the living room carrying plates and cutlery. 'There are carp in the pond in summer,' she says, straight-faced.

'Carp?' I can't keep the squeak of disbelief out of my voice.

Tanya and her mother burst out laughing. 'Not really, no carp. Just crap. Crap all year round,' says Tanya. It's not the first time her humour has caught me out.

The living-room walls are lined with books, some in English and French. 'Studying is a way of life for us,' says Julka. She's a retired teacher and admits to listening to the BBC World Service back when it was banned. Next to Dickens, Hugo and Shakespeare, there's an Edward Said paperback: *Culture and Imperialism*. Olga is doing an MBA at Moscow State.

'Moscow State University, that's where you should go. I could fix a scholarship through the unions,' says my uncle. It's 1966. I've just moved into the sixth form.

'Bugger that. Your headmistress tells me you're bright enough for Oxford,' says my father, when I write and tell him what my uncle has said.

'Oxford, then Moscow State, you wouldn't be the first,' says my uncle. I like the idea of Oxford. I'm not sure about Moscow

State, but I don't tell my uncle that. After years of bouncing between his idealistic politics and my father's hedonistic lifestyle, I'm beginning to filter what I say to them both. It's a skill I've kept with me into adulthood.

Family photographs crowd the bookshelves: Julka's husband, bare-armed and stocky, sitting under a plum tree outside their dacha; Tanya's husband, in military uniform, round-faced, full-lipped (he was killed in Afghanistan); Olga, a toothy baby on her father's knee.

The three women sitting on the sofa in front of the bookshelves all have the same high cheekbones and brown eyes, but Olga has her father's mouth. As I look across at them, I get a lump in my throat. At first, I can't work out why.

'Think of the history sitting on that sofa,' my uncle pipes up. Maybe that's partly it: grandmother born when Lenin was in power, daughter born the year Stalin died, granddaughter living more of her life after Communism than under it. Three generations of women and their men behind them in the photographs, stretching over the century. But it's not so much the history, it's their sense of family, still close, still part of each other's lives. That's what moves me.

Lunch is pierogi (vegetable pie) and ploff (spiced lamb and rice), followed by bottled plums from the dacha. Olga ignores the plums, cuts some white bread and spreads Nutella on it. Early afternoon, we decide to go back into Moscow, to Red

Square. Olga wants to see the new Revlon counter at GUM, now *the* department store for Russians with spending power. She changes into her denims. Julka's not coming with us. Moscow's no place for the old these days, she says, but she gives her grand-daughter some roubles to treat herself. As we leave, she kisses me on the cheek and says I must visit again, we'll talk more about the old Russia. The lump in my throat comes back.

I like her, and I'm not good at goodbyes.

Red Square isn't square, it's bent-out-of-shape rectangular. It's not as vast as it appeared on those sixties May Day newsreels, and the balcony where all the party leaders stood is only about twenty feet off the ground, not as high as it looked back then. Of all those grim-faced old men loaded with medals who stood there waving and saluting, I can only remember Khrushchev.

'Bloody peasant, he's taken us all to the brink.' My father is trying to tune the radio, cursing the poor reception but mostly cursing Khrushchev. October 1962, and I'm with my father for half-term, in a rented cottage in Wales. The Cuban crisis has been ratcheting up all week, and he spends every evening searching for 'Voice of America' on the radio or fiddling with the silvery aerial feelers on top of the juddery TV, so he can watch the news. We listen to President Kennedy's speech. He pronounces Khrushchev as Kroo-shof and says the Soviets have nuclear missiles in Cuba that could strike against the Western Hemisphere.

My father explains to me that this is dangerous but says I shouldn't worry.

On Saturday, we go to the village, but there's scarcely anyone around, and the shopkeepers seem in a hurry to close up. About eight o'clock in the evening, my father switches off the radio and starts to talk to me. What am I reading? Is it good? What do I want to do when I leave school? He might have to go to Quebec next summer. Would I like to go with him? Then he says he's sorry he's had to send me back to school in the UK, he misses me, but it was the only way I could get a decent education.

It's the first time he's talked to me like this, and it feels strange, this grown-up way of doing things. He keeps making me cups of cocoa as the evening goes on. About midnight, he says maybe I should go to bed. I can't sleep. Every noise is a May Day missile. I get up to go to the toilet and see my father asleep in his armchair, the radio crackling beside him. I wake him up, and he says, 'Go back to bed, you'll get cold.' He hugs me.

Sunday morning, he brings me a cup of tea in bed and tells me 'Voice of America' says Khrushchev has broadcast on Radio Moscow: the weapons in Cuba will be dismantled. He tickles my feet and tells me we're going out for lunch. Sunday evening, he drops me back at my uncle's house. Friday, he leaves for Barbados. The whole of that week, my uncle never mentions Cuba.

I press my bare palm against the freezing brick of the Kremlin Wall and run my finger over the plaque, picking out the name in the Cyrillic alphabet.

'He was my hero, Yuri Gagarin,' says Tanya.

'He was everyone's hero.'

'He's a foundry man, and he likes Manchester,' says my uncle. July 1961, three months after Yuri's space flight. My uncle's fixed it so we can see him at Trafford Park where the Union of Foundry Workers has arranged for him to visit. Yuri's bright-green uniform almost glows among the grey suits and drab overalls. He's small, towered over by the men around him, but my uncle explains he has to be, to fit in the space capsule. 'Yuri! Yuri!' We all shout. Later, he goes by in the motor parade, and we get a good view of him because he refuses to put the hood of his car up.

He thanks the people of Manchester for waiting in the rain to welcome him and wins everyone over with that sunburst of a smile.

Even my father is impressed when I write and tell him I saw Yuri. 'The first man in space, it's unbelievable,' he writes back.

I don't tell him I waved the Red Flag.

Tanya touches Yuri's plaque. 'He showed us anything is possible, but he had integrity, values. Even now he means so much. For us, he represents the old Russia.'

Julka talked about old Russia too. And I realise they don't mean pre-Revolution Russia, that's what I call old Russia, they mean the Russia before Communism fell.

'I wonder what he'd say if he'd lived to see the changes?' I say.

'Perhaps it's better he didn't, though it broke all our hearts when he died.'

27 March 1968. I'm in Caernarvon, on a university study trip. I'm at Manchester University. I didn't get to Oxford. My father thinks it's because of my uncle's influence. I know it's because I didn't work hard enough. I still filter their comments, but I'm enjoying the freedom of not having to answer to either of them any more. Just before we leave the study centre, we hear on the radio about Gagarin's plane crash. All the way back, each news bulletin on the bus radio gives more updates. The Soviets are being tight-lipped, but the whole of Moscow seems to be out on the streets in mourning.

My father hasn't come to see me this Easter, so I'm staying with a friend. There's a telegram waiting for me, the first one I've ever had addressed to me personally. It's from my father's woman friend. It says my father has died. He's had a massive coronary, back in Barbados.

I can't take it in.

I don't go back for the funeral in Barbados. I never go back.

I spend the next two years in free fall.

Somehow, I manage to get a decent Manchester degree. On Graduation Day, I wonder if my father would have been pleased or disappointed.

'It's a good university, Manchester,' says my uncle, on the day. There's a slight hesitancy – I can feel him struggling – but he manages it, he manages not to say, 'but it's not Moscow State.'

Years later, I do go to Oxford, as a postgraduate. By then, my uncle is dead too. On this second graduation day, sitting in the Sheldonian in Oxford, I think back to my uncle's sofa and the spats about the Soviets going on over my head.

Now I'm here in Russia, teaching students from Moscow State. My father and uncle are still with me. Do both of them finally approve? So much to argue with them about, so much to thank them for. But they stand quiet.

I trace Yuri's dates with my finger: 1934–1968. And the tears come.

Tanya doesn't say anything. She waits a while, then slips her arm in mine, and we make our way across Red Square towards GUM to meet Olga.

THE GRAVEDIGGER

HELENA KILTY

I arrive at the farm as the sun is setting and unpack everything I'll need from the boot of the car: a bale of straw, a pair of heavy gardening gloves, a roll of thick black plastic, a pickaxe and a small shovel.

As soon as I finish unloading the car, the door of the Irish farmhouse opens. My host, Carmel, emerges, skirt billowing around her ankles, long blonde hair freshly washed and still damp.

'Welcome,' she says, gathering me to her, so my head is somewhere between her enormous bosom and her soft face. 'Let me show you where you'll be going.'

This will be my first initiation with medicine woman Carmel, part Cherokee Indian. We head into the cold night, the earth squelching under our feet, until we reach a field. She points to a spot towards the back of the field, indicating I should dig here.

'It has to be the same as any other grave,' she says.

I nod, grateful that my small frame means I only have to make it five foot five inches long, and grateful too that I have one more sleep left.

When we get back to the house, I eat supper. There won't be any more food until the deed is done. Knowing that my body's reaction to fasting is to vomit, I eat light. I have some pieces of roast chicken and three slices of goat's cheese, followed by a steaming mug of tea. In spite of my inclination to stay up chatting, I know I'll need my sleep, so I head to bed. In the morning, I will rise with the sun to dig my own grave.

The alarm goes off at four-fifty. I pull on layers of warm clothes. As soon as I'm standing on the gravel, the sun comes up over the mountain. Initially the hues of pink are barely visible but then the colour intensifies, turning orange, spreading out across the skyline. I gather my tools, hope I have the energy to carry this off and head out to the field. I have until sundown to dig the hole.

Where to start? I've never been much of a gardener. I know very little about digging earth, though common sense tells me not to dig near any ant colonies. No sign of ants here. The ground is covered in scrub. I find a patch that looks easy and begin to scrape away the weeds. There are loads of them. It quickly becomes frustrating. Every time I put the shovel into the ground, the weeds get in the way. Finally I realise the ground is almost frozen solid. It will take me a long time to dig this thing.

Clearly, the best way to proceed is to remove only the top layer of soil and work from there. The plan works.

I keep digging. My hands become blistered, in spite of gardening gloves. My arms ache. My back aches. I'm tired. The hole is not yet shin deep. I feel like I've been digging for days, but the sun is still rising.

I put down the shovel. Brandon, Carmel's black Labrador mix, arrives. He has his favourite squeaky duck with him, and he wants to play.

'Can't play now, too busy.'

He looks at me defiantly and flings the yellow duck into the hole. I pick it up and throw it for him. He's delighted and bounds off to get it. When he returns, I've gone back to digging.

He flings Ducky at me again and paws the ground. I ignore him. He gets into the grave with me. Ducky, Brandon and myself have a stand-off. I'm happy to have some company, but I can't play and dig at the same time. Brandon's just as stubborn as I am. Also, he knows if he's patient, I'll give in. I throw the thing again. After what seems like ages, Brandon gets fed up and heads off.

I think about my young family and hope they'll sleep easy tonight. I think about my husband and know that they're safe. He'd never have agreed to this before, but when I'd mentioned it to him last month, he'd agreed easily. 'We just need you to come back to us,' he'd said, and I'd felt the familiar sense of guilt settle in my bones.

I go back to focusing on the task at hand. One day, some-one will be doing this for me. Who will those men be? I think about their arms, their backs. I say a prayer that the earth is soft for them. I say a prayer for their families. I thank them for their hard graft.

At twilight, Carmel comes to see how I'm getting on. She takes a look at my grave and reckons I'm almost there. Just a few more inches and it'll be ready. However, I've hit a big rock, right where my head will go. I can't dig around it. I heave and push and pull and plead with the thing to move, but it won't budge. Finally, we decide I can make the grave longer at the other end, to make up for it. Stepping back to admire my handiwork, I look in. I've dug a very large and deep hole for myself. All I need to do now is line it with straw so I won't be lying directly against damp soil.

Just before six o'clock, I head back to the main house to get ready. I pull on more layers of clothes: a couple of Merino-wool vests and some jumpers, a pair of grey woollen leggings, navy tracksuit bottoms and a pair of waterproof trousers. At sunset, I will get in, cover myself with heavy black plastic and remain there for the night.

Spending the night with mice or rats is not appealing – though I'm not fond of creepy-crawlies either (ticks in particu-lar). However, I get in and pull the tarpaulin over the grave. I'm plunged into complete blackness.

An old friend once told me about camping as a child and waking in the night to find hundreds of ants crawling on the roof of her tent. I reach my hand up to feel along the tarpaulin. The plastic is insect-free. Maybe the ants are waiting. Then they will head for my face first, next, intimate parts of my body.

I begin to sweat. I should have cheated and made the grave bigger than necessary so I'd have room to move. I am completely hemmed in. I wiggle out of my rain jacket. I'm still too hot. I need to take off my jumper, which is trickier, but I manage it. I hope the temperature won't drop later in the night.

The task is to feed to death all that gets in the way of living fully. To do this, I need to stay awake. And be present to whatever comes, even if it is ants. My body begins to shake. At first it is gentle, but then it becomes more pronounced.

I'm surprised that an ex-boyfriend springs to mind. The evening we broke up, we'd had dinner with friends. On the way home, he'd asked should we end things. I wasn't surprised. We hadn't made love in over twelve months. I wanted to say it was nothing at all to do with him. I wanted to tell him that a cloak of blackness had settled itself around me and I couldn't shake it off, but I sat there silently. Eventually I told him we should do whatever he thought was best. In spite of the three and a half years, when he nodded and said, 'I think we should leave it at that,' I felt nothing. The entire relationship plays itself out; all the moments I left him wondering what the hell was going on with me. I'm left with a knot in my belly, recognition that I was scared of getting too close. I'll ring him when I get out, and apologise.

The grass rustles. I hold my breath. Is it a colony of giant ants? The rustling gets closer.

The night in America when an acquaintance spiked my drink suddenly flashes at me. The numbness waited till I was in the taxi and crept up my legs and into my hips, all in one go. An image comes, of me perplexed at the sensation of partial paralysis; the taxi driver catching my eye in the rear-view mirror. From the distance of a decade, it's easy to recognise the tone of resignation in his insistence that he wants no part in any of this. Another one, of me laughing at him, still innocent then; sure aren't they taking me home? I begin to sweat again. The shaking becomes more violent, until it feels as though the grave itself is shaking. He's most likely still in Cape Cod or some other part of America. It was a long time ago. The chances that he's in a field in Kildare are slim. Nonetheless, some form of paw or foot pounds the earth firmly. Brandon has been locked in for the night. The few other people that know I'm here will not come near me until morning. There are no tigers or bears in Ireland, not even in Kildare, but the grass is being pounded by something heavy. Not knowing if it's the middle of the night or still evening, I prepare myself for the possibility that a stray walker, or worse, may stumble across the grave and fall in.

The rustling is almost upon me. My heart beats quickly and fiercely. For a very brief moment I hear the sound of a second heartbeat. Something snorts. It's not a human sound. I hold my breath. After a few moments, whatever it is begins to move away, leaving me alone again. There are cows in the next field. Perhaps one of them escaped.

My skin is clammy, and nausea rises from my belly. The straw, scratchy against my bare neck, smells as though it's been lying in a corner of a stable for the past number of weeks (which it has). I press my face against the earthen wall, letting the pleasant smell of damp clay waft up my nostrils.

With my head resting on the slab of stone I couldn't move earlier and the right side of my face pressed against the soil, I begin to cool down. I'm reminded of those familiar lines, 'Ashes to ashes, dust to dust.' And then it comes, like I knew it would.

It begins always at the same moment. I'm in the car. Rain hits the bonnet in thick dense sheets. He really does appear from nowhere. There's a heavy thump-thud of weight against bumper. People who know about these things say everything slows down, and they're right. There's enough time to think I imagined it. Then comes the fracturing of windscreen; he hurtles through glass, as though someone's picked him up and flung him right at me. There's the back of his head, the soft folds of neck, a left arm, crook of elbow. In spite of this, there's an instant of thinking I've hit a deer, a brief moment where things might still be all right.

The traction of the glass causes him to bounces backwards, so that he lands face down on wet tarmac. I call an ambulance, but they tell me it'll take forty minutes to reach us. Liquid dribbles from his right ear. Eventually he starts to breathe. He gulps air thickly, as though, having spent time at the bottom of an ocean, he's now risen to the surface. I hold his hand and peer closely at his profile. If I manage to keep him alive till the ambulance arrives, surely they can keep him alive after that? After a minute, he starts to move and tries to get his broken body up off the ground. Should I let him stand up? Blood oozes stickily from the top of his head. His elderly face is smashed and concave. *I did this to you*, I think. *I did this to you.*

At the funeral, the priest makes sure to say that he'd known death was coming for him. 'Without immediate family, he was afraid of dying alone,' the priest says, before looking into the pews to hold my gaze; 'well, we can be grateful he was not alone when death finally came.' I wrap the oversized woollen coat around me, more for protection than for heat; the church is surprisingly humid. He's trying to alleviate my guilt. I feel numb.

Outside the church, his god-daughter shakes my hand and thanks me for coming. She knows this must be difficult, but it means a lot to them, she says, before adding that he'd taken to getting confused and wandering out at night. My face hurts then, from the effort of not crying.

The heat has spread to my whole body. Nausea rises again; the muscles in my stomach contract. I roll over to my side and rest my head at the top of the grave. Acrid bile; is that noise coming from me? A wail rises from my belly and rolls through me.

My heart thumps strongly. The earth holds me, safe. Some form of creepy-crawly moves steadily beside my left eye; its legs make a tiny click-click as they go forward. There is a second heartbeat in the grave now, pressing my ear further into the moist clay, it sounds as though it's coming from deep within the molten core. My own heartbeat tries to match it. Then it is gone, only mine remains. If I travel through the blame, what's on the other side? I cry out. I'm not sure I believe in God. Is that who I'm calling to now?

I remember a story I was told once, that at the moment of death our heart will be placed carefully on a weighing scale. If we have lived well, it will be in balance. If we have not, it will be either too light or too heavy. I have been wearing guilt and shame like a second skin, since long before the accident. I've been wearing it my entire life. I can't keep living like this. This is not life.

Eventually my breathing settles. I imagine my body dissolving, decomposing; the creepy-crawlies I'm avoiding take tiny pieces of my body, carrying me off to wherever they go. I imagine the worms eating me, taking me in as one thing, passing me out as something else. My body starts to shake, and the sweating comes again. This time, I just go with it. The cells of my body start to tingle, oscillating at their own unique frequency. I'm acutely aware of my skin, the way it hangs on my bones, bends and expands as I move my knee towards the wall of the grave.

These arms pick up my children, hold them dearly. These hips carry them from room to room. These strong legs walk the prom in Salthill, the wind blowing rain into my face, leaving traces of salt along my cheeks, on my lips. This body dances to Bob Dylan at home in my kitchen, bare feet enjoying contact with the smooth lino floor; it enjoys making love. I want more of all that.

The birds begin to move restlessly in the trees above me, getting ready for second dawn. Finally, I hear Carmel's voice. 'The night is over. I welcome you into the first day of your new life.'

I stand up and look around me. The sun is rising again over the mountain.

THE HEALER

DEREK FLYNN

No one knew for sure how the house – if that was the right word for it – had appeared on the beach. They'd simply woken up and it was there. Mikey Bolger said he'd heard the banging in the middle of the night, but no one else had, and no one really took too much notice of Mikey.

All they knew for sure was that the day before it had been a pile of junk, and today it was something that – if you were feeling generous – could be called a 'dwelling'.

The junk had started to appear a month before. At first, it was just some old planks of wood, mouldy and water-damaged, that looked like they had washed up on the beach. But as the wood pile increased in size, the locals started to realise it was something more. They wondered if someone was building a bonfire, but Halloween was months away, and pretty soon other items began to accumulate that put paid to that idea: hubcaps, fluorescent beer signs, an armchair and even a life-size cardboard cut-out of Sean Connery that looked like it had come from a cinema or a video store.

But no one had seen who it was leaving all the junk there. The Worm said it was like the old fairy story about the elves that came in the night to do the shoemaker's work for him. But nobody really believed that elves were doing the work.

Except, maybe, Mikey Bolger.

Each day, Joe Ryan, out for his daily constitutional, would walk along the beach and scour the junk pile for any newly added oddities. That night, in the Wreck bar, Joe and the other locals would compare notes and advance their latest theories on who was responsible and why.

And then, one day, it stopped.

There were no new additions to the pile. For three days, it sat there, as bemused locals took their walks and stood staring at the junk pile as though it was a trick, as though they had somehow been duped. The rumour mill went into overdrive as people speculated as to what could have happened. Aliens were even mentioned at one stage.

But again, that was probably Mikey Bolger.

The sense of curiosity that had gripped the village of Ardmore Bay slowly turned to a kind of panic. No one said as much, but you could see they were missing their mysterious night figure and his deposits of scrap. What if that was it? What if it was over and the person was never coming back? What then?

Would there never be an explanation?

The pile lay there for weeks, never moving. No matter how far the tide came in, not one piece of the pile moved from the spot it had been placed in.

'How's that possible?' Shamie asked Conn, the barman, one night. 'That the tide never washes away the rubbish?'

From the other side of the bar came Mikey Bolger's voice. 'Ah sure, 'tis physics, isn't it?'

'How's that?' Shamie said.

Mikey was what people liked to call a 'lean streak of misery': tall and gangly, with the added misfortune of a neck almost as long as his legs. He was also not the brightest bulb in the box. As Conn was often heard to comment, 'You'd think, the size of him, they'd have managed to fit a bit more brain in.' Mikey craned his long neck and looked blankly at Shamie for a moment, finally giving up and dropping his head again.

'I'll tell ya who'd know that now,' Conn said. 'The Worm.'

Shamie nodded his head vigorously. 'Oh, the Worm'd know all right.'

The Worm had gotten his nickname not because he was shifty or untrustworthy in any way but because he read books. As it turned out, Shamie never got to ask the Worm, because the next day, the village woke to see that the junk pile had been turned into a house. The door and window were plastic sheeting, the beer signs had been hung all the way around the walls, and Sean Connery stood outside the door as though guarding it.

Joe Ryan made sure that his walk that morning took him past the hut. As he approached, he saw a man sitting outside the doorway. At first glance, Joe thought he might be a tramp.

'Morning,' the man said.

Joe put his hand to the peak of his soft cap. 'Mornin'.'

As he studied the man's face, Joe changed his mind. Despite a few days' worth of stubble, it didn't look like a face that had been exposed to the elements.

'Looks like it could be a nice day,' the man said.

'Weather forecast is good,' Joe replied, having come to a halt. He felt his heart pumping a little faster. So this was the architect, the mysterious elf. He wanted to run back to the village, wake everyone up out of bed and tell them.

'Won't you sit down?' the man said.

Joe looked around warily, as though he was doing something wrong, and then felt stupid having done it. He sat down, wincing as he did so.

'You okay?' the man asked.

'It's the gout. Givin' me an awful time.' Sean Connery was glaring down at him.

'Terrible thing,' the man said, rooting around in the bag beside him. He took out a small bottle of clear liquid and offered it to Joe.

'Try this,' he said.

Joe shook his head. 'Ah, it's a bit early for me.'

'For the gout. Try it.'

Joe put out his hand cautiously and took the bottle. Opening it, he took a quick swig.

'Jaysus! Tastes like dishwater.'

The man smiled. 'Couple of days,' he said, 'you'll be right as rain.'

Joe told all those assembled in the Wreck that night about his meeting with the man and the concoction he had given him.

'And didya drink it?' Shamie asked, doing little to hide his disgust.

'Of course I did.'

'But sure it could be anythin' …'

'Not at all. That man knows what he's talkin' about. Sure, he's obviously one of them "fate" healers.'

The Worm was sitting over a pint of stout. 'Reminds me of a story about this Greek philosopher from ancient times,' he said. 'Forget his name. He was the wisest man that ever lived, but he lived like a tramp. Wore rags, slept in a cardboard box …'

'Did they have cardboard in them days?' Shamie asked.

'Well, I dunno, a wooden box then. Anyway, one day Alexander the Great came to see him. He told the philosopher who he was and how he'd conquered the known world and how he commanded mighty armies and had untold wealth and riches, and he asks the philosopher, "Is there anythin' I can do for you? Just name it." And the philosopher says, "Yeah, move a little to the left. You're blocking me light."'

There was silence around the bar for a moment, and then Shamie said, 'That's the stupidest joke I ever heard.'

'It's not a fecking joke,' the Worm said. 'It's a story.'

'Well … stupid story.'

'Jaysus, ye haven't an ounce of culture between the lot of ye.'

After three days, Joe announced to anyone who would listen how much better he was feeling. As soon as he said it, the floodgates were opened. By that evening, there was a queue of villagers snaking its way along the beach and up to the man's hut.

There was Brendan with his arthritis, Maureen with her corns, Stephen with his haemorrhoids. The whole village seemed to be there. And the healer agreed to help every one of them as best he could, asking only one thing in return: that they tell no one outside the village about him.

Of course, everyone agreed that this would not be a problem.

Three weeks later, word got out.

They started coming slowly: a few cars pulling up in the village on a Sunday afternoon, their passengers taking a walk along the beach and gaping at the hut. Most simply passed it off, but one or two lingered and knocked on the door.

The healer never answered. It was as if he knew they were outsiders.

At first, neither he nor the villagers mentioned the new visitors; they simply carried on as normal: patients and physician. But, before long, it couldn't be ignored any more. The numbers were increasing, and on weekends the villagers could barely get out of their houses with the cars parked all around. The outsiders' curiosity was aroused even more by the occasional loose tongue in the village describing miraculous cures.

The healer had given up answering the door to any of them now. Occasionally he could be seen through the plastic sheeting, looking more disappointed than angry.

Matters got worse with the arrival of a group of young men and women with long hair and tie-dye T-shirts, who used the words 'guru' and 'shaman' when referring to the man and sat outside the hut day and night singing and chanting.

One morning, when they woke, the door to the hut was open. They looked at each other anxiously, until finally one of them tiptoed up to it and peered inside. It didn't take long for word to reach the village.

The healer was gone.

But, even then, they didn't leave. They started to treat the hut as though it were some kind of shrine, laying offerings outside and praying for the return of their 'saviour'. Joe watched them every morning as he went for his walk, and he was amazed. Not a single one of them had ever met the man or been affected by him, yet they all believed that he would save them in some way.

The entire village could see the breaking point coming, and when it did, no one was surprised. One Saturday night, after closing time, Conn was walking home from the Wreck when he heard a commotion on the beach.

In the distance he could see the hut in flames.

He walked down towards the beach and could see all the outsiders scrambling to try and put out the fire. But it was no use. It had gone up like a tinder stick, and by morning there was nothing left but ash and melted plastic.

Over the next few days, the outsiders drifted away, bit by bit, until there was no one and nothing left on the beach. Even the remains of the hut were washed away. Life in the village went back to normal: quiet resumed, the traffic disappeared, and all the old ailments and sicknesses gradually returned.

One morning, months later, Joe was on his morning walk when he saw a familiar figure on the beach. He stopped beside the man and eased himself down slowly onto the ground.

'The gout at you again, Joe?' the man asked.

'Ah sure … you know yourself.'

'Want me to give you something for it?'

Joe smiled and shook his head. 'I don't think so. Sure, you won't be stoppin', so I'll have to get used to life without it sooner or later. Might as well be sooner.'

They were silent for a moment, as the waves lapped gently at the sand.

'Sorry for what happened to your house,' Joe said.

'It's only a few planks of wood. I'm sorry for what happened to your town.'

Joe glanced over his shoulder back at the village. 'Ah, they'll live.'

When he turned back, the man was standing and reaching his hand out.

'It was nice meeting you,' he said. 'Maybe we'll run into each other again.'

Joe stood also and shook his hand. 'I'll be here.'

He watched as the man started down the beach in the direction of the rocks. It was the same route Joe took every day. When you reached a certain point, the water came in over the rocks and you had to turn back. For a second, Joe wondered where the man was going. He contemplated waiting around to see if the man would turn back, but decided against it and walked back to the village.

CONTRIBUTORS

FRANK MCGUINNESS

Frank McGuinness is Professor of Creative Writing in University College Dublin. A world-renowned playwright, his works include *Observe the Sons of Ulster Marching Towards the Somme, The Factory Girls, Someone Who'll Watch Over Me* and, most recently, *The Hanging Gardens*. The author of acclaimed novel, *Arimathea*, and several anthologies of poetry, he is also a highly skilled adapter of plays by writers such as Ibsen, Sophocles, Brecht, and writer of a number of film scripts, including *Dancing at Lughnasa*. He wrote the libretto for Julian Anderson's opera *Thebans*, produced by the English National Opera, which premiered at the London Coliseum in 2014.

COLIN CORRIGAN

Colin Corrigan was born in Co. Kildare and lives in Ann Arbor, Michigan. He has an MA in Creative Writing from UCD and is currently pursuing an MFA at the Helen Zell Writers' Program at the University of Michigan. Two short films he wrote (one of which he directed) have screened internationally at festivals and have been broadcast on RTÉ. His short fiction has appeared in the *Stinging Fly*, *The Fiction Desk* and Amazon's weekly literary journal, *Day One*.

FERGUS CRONIN

Fergus Cronin grew up in Dublin in the 1950s and 1960s. He qualified with a BE from UCD in 1972 and worked as an actor and an engineer. In 1979 he moved to Kilkenny, where he spent twenty-five years working in water treatment and raising two wonderful girls. In 2004, he moved to north Connemara to pursue his enduring interests in the worlds of media, theatre and literature. He has been deeply involved in many educational and cultural initiatives in the city, including the Kilkenny Arts Festival, the Cat Laughs Comedy Festival, KCLR and the Kilkenny School Project.

MADELEINE D'ARCY

Madeleine D'Arcy worked as a criminal legal-aid solicitor and as a legal editor in London before returning to Cork in 1999 with her husband and son. She began to write short stories in 2005. In 2010, she received a Hennessy X.O. Literary Award for First Fiction as well as the overall Hennessy X.O. Literary Award for New Irish Writer. Madeleine's story 'Dog Pound' has been made into a short film, starring Frank Kelly. Her short-story collection, *Waiting for the Bullet*, was published by Doire Press in April 2014. She is a student on the inaugural master's degree in creative writing at UCC.

DEREK FLYNN

Derek Flynn is an Irish writer and musician. He has been published in a number of publications, including the *Irish Times*, and was first runner-up for the J. G. Farrell Award for Best Novel-in-Progress. Derek is a regular contributor to Writing.ie, where he writes his 'Songbook' column and interviews writers and musicians. He released his third album, *Debris*, in May 2014. He can be found online at http://derekflynn.wordpress.com.

HELENA KILTY

Helena Kilty grew up in Skerries, Co. Dublin. For the past twelve years, she's lived in Galway, where she divides her time between writing and working as a psychotherapist. She is working on a collection of short stories. She also writes non-fiction. She's a member of the Galway Writers' Workshop and completed the MA in writing at NUI Galway in 2012. Her work has been published in *Skylight47*, *Crannóg* and the *Abandoned Darlings* anthology.

SHEILA LLEWELLYN

Sheila Llewellyn did the MA in creative writing at the Seamus Heaney Centre, Queen's, in 2011–12. She is now doing a Ph.D. there, in creative writing, and finishing off her first novel. In 2011, she won the RTÉ Radio One P. J. O'Connor Award for Radio Drama. She was shortlisted for the Costa Short Story Award in 2012 and in 2013. She has also been shortlisted for the Bridport Short Story Prize, the Bridport Flash Fiction Prize, the Seán Ó Faoláin Prize and the Fish Short Memoir Prize. She has read at the Ulster Hall 'Literary Lunchtime' events and at the Word Factory 'Short Story Salon' at Waterstones, Piccadilly, London.

DARRAN MCCANN

Darran McCann is from Armagh. He was educated at TCD and at Dublin City University. He worked as a journalist and had work published in local and national newspapers and magazines throughout Ireland and the UK before becoming a news re-porter on the staff of Belfast's *Irish News*. He went on to earn an MA, then a Ph.D., in creative writing at Queen's – the latter be-ing the first time a doctorate in creative writing had ever been awarded by an Irish university. His play, *Confession*, was pro-duced by Accidental Theatre at the Brian Friel Theatre, Belfast, in 2008. His debut novel, *After the Lockout*, was published by Fourth Estate in 2012.

MIKE MCCORMACK

Mike McCormack is the author of two collections of short stories, *Getting It in the Head* and *Forensic Songs*, and two novels, *Crowe's Requiem* and *Notes from a Coma*. In 1996, he was awarded the Rooney Prize for Irish Literature, and *Getting It in the Head* was chosen as a New York Times Notable Book. In 2006, *Notes from a Coma* was shortlisted for the Irish Book of the Year Award; it was recently published by SOHO Press in New York. He was awarded a Civitella Ranieri Fellowship in 2007, and he has been the recipient of several Arts Council bursaries.

PAULA MCGRATH

Paula McGrath is finishing her MFA at UCD, where her thesis is a novel in stories called *No One's from Chicago*. She is represented by Ger Nichol, and her novel, *Michaelangelos*, is currently on submission. Her work has appeared in *Necessary Fiction*, *Mslexia*, *ROPES Galway* and other publications; she was recently shortlisted for the inaugural Maeve Binchy Travel Award and longlisted for the Penguin Ireland/RTÉ Guide Short Story Competition in 2013.

MARY MORRISSY

Mary Morrissy is the author of a collection of short stories, *A Lazy Eye*, and three novels, *Mother of Pearl*, *The Pretender* and, most recently, *The Rising of Bella Casey*. She is among the contributors to Tramp Press's *Dubliners 100*, celebrating the centenary of Joyce's *Dubliners*. Her volume of short stories, *Diaspora*, is forthcoming. Her short fiction has won a Hennessy Award, and, in 1995, she was awarded the prestigious Lannan Literary Award for Fiction. She has been nominated for the International IMPAC Dublin Literary Award and shortlisted for the Whitbread (now Costa) Book Award. She has taught creative writing in Ireland and in the USA for the past fourteen years. She currently leads the fiction component of the MA in creative writing at UCC. Her website on fiction and history is at marymorrissy.wordpress.com.

GINA MOXLEY

Gina Moxley is a writer, actor and theatre director. Her stage plays have been produced nationally and internationally. She was winner of the Stewart Parker New Playwright Bursary for her first play, *Danti-Dan*, produced by Rough Magic in 1995. Both *Danti-Dan* and *Dog House* were published by Faber, and *The Crumb Trail*, produced by Pan Pan, was chosen as one of the best contemporary European plays by the European Theatre Convention in 2010. She has also written several plays for radio, broadcast by RTÉ. Some of her short stories have been published by the *Stinging Fly*, and she was a contributor to *Yeats Is Dead!*, a novel by fifteen Irish writers.

ÉILÍS NÍ DHUIBHNE

Éilís Ní Dhuibhne was born in Dublin. She has written eight novels, six collections of short stories, several books for children, plays and non-fiction work. Her short-story collections include *Midwife to the Fairies*, *The Inland Ice*, *The Pale Gold of Alaska* and *The Shelter of Neighbours*. Among her novels are *Cailíní Beaga Ghleann na mBláth*, *Hurlamaboc*, *Dúnmharú sa Daingean*, *The Dancers Dancing* and *Fox, Swallow, Scarecrow*. She has received numerous literary awards, including the Bisto Book of the Year Award, the Reading Association of Ireland Children's Book Award, the Stewart Parker Award for Drama, the Butler Award for Prose from the Irish American Cultural Institute and several Oireachtas awards for novels in Irish. *The Dancers Dancing* was shortlisted for the Orange Prize for Fiction. Her stories are widely anthologised and translated. Éilís was for many years a curator in the National Library of Ireland. She teaches creative writing in UCD and is a member of Aosdána.

RUTH QUINLAN

Ruth Quinlan is from Tralee, Co. Kerry, and holds an MA in Writing from NUI Galway. She won the Hennessy X.O. Literary Award for First Fiction in 2013 and was shortlisted for the 2012 and 2014 Cúirt New Writing Prize. Her work has been published by the *Irish Independent*, *ROPES*, *Crannóg*, *Skylight47*, *Emerge Literary Journal*, *Thresholds* and *Scissors & Spackle*; she has also contributed both fiction and poetry to several anthologies. Recently, she joined the editing team of *Skylight47*, a poetry magazine based in Galway.

CLAIRE SIMPSON

Claire Simpson is originally from north Antrim. She read English at TCD and creative writing at Queen's. Her work has been published in *Crannóg* and on Spontaneity.org. She is studying for a Ph.D. at the Seamus Heaney Centre and lives in Belfast.

BRIDGET SPROULS

Bridget Sprouls is from New Jersey. Her poems and stories have appeared in the *Belleville Park Pages*, *Steps Magazine*, *Scrivener Creative Review*, *Casino*, *The Red Wheelbarrow Poets Anthology* and the *McGill Daily*. In 2013, her work was shortlisted for the Atlantic Writing Prize in the categories of Short Fiction and Writing for Children.

UNIVERSITIES

NATIONAL UNIVERSITY OF IRELAND, GALWAY

Mike McCormack (Fiction Tutor)

Helena Kilty

Ruth Quinlan

QUEEN'S UNIVERSITY BELFAST

Dr Darran McCann (Creative Writing Lecturer)

Sheila Llewellyn

Claire Simpson

TRINITY COLLEGE DUBLIN

Gina Moxley (Creative Writing Graduate)

Fergus Cronin

Derek Flynn

UNIVERSITY COLLEGE DUBLIN

Professor Frank McGuinness (Writer-in-Residence)

Dr Éilís Ní Dhuibhne (Fellow in Creative Writing)

Colin Corrigan

Paula McGrath

UNIVERSITY COLLEGE CORK

Mary Morrissy (Writer Fellow)

Madeleine D'Arcy

Bridget Sprouls